Confidentially YOURS

Vanessa's Design Dilemma

ALSO BY JO WHITTEMORE

Confidentially Yours #1: Brooke's Not-So-Perfect Plan

Confidentially Yours #2: Vanessa's Fashion Face-Off

Confidentially Yours #3: Heather's Crush Catastrophe

Confidentially Yours #4: The Secret Talent

Confidentially Yours #5: Brooke's Bad Luck

JO WHITTEMORE

Confidentially YOURS

Vanessa's Design Dilemma

6

HARPER
An Imprint of HarperCollinsPublishers

Confidentially Yours: Vanessa's Design Dilemma
 For information address HarperCollins Children's Books, a division of HarperCollins Publishers, 195 Broadway, New York, NY 10007.
www.harpercollinschildrens.com

Library of Congress Control Number: 2017932843
ISBN 978-0-06-235903-2

Typography by Kate J. Engbring
17 18 19 20 21 OPM 10 9 8 7 6 5 4 3 2 1

First Edition

Confidentially YOURS

Vanessa's Design Dilemma

Contents

CHAPTER

1

Unconfidentially Yours

"Major disaster! End of the world!" Katie Kestler sprinted toward me, waving her hands over her head.

I lifted an eyebrow but didn't join the panic. . . . Mostly because it's not my style, but also because I'd recently bought a cute sweater. The world wasn't allowed to end until I'd worn it at least twice.

"What's going on?" I asked.

"And how can you run in those shoes?" added Tim Antonides, peering at Katie's heeled boots.

He was sitting beside me at lunch, along with

my other best friends Brooke Jacobs and Heather Schwartz.

"I actually can't." Katie's panicked expression turned into a pained one, and she dropped into a nearby chair. As she bent to inspect one of her boots, she placed a fabric scrap on our table.

Brooke picked it up.

"I'm guessing the major disaster has to do with this red cloth," she said. "That, or you've started miniature bullfighting."

"No, you had it right the first time," Katie said, straightening. "The cloth is the wrong shade of red. Vanessa and I ordered crimson." She took the swatch from Brooke and held it up for my inspection.

"Oh no. Poppy?" I clapped a hand to my forehead. "What happened to *our* fabric?"

Katie and I are the future of fashion. When she moved in across the street a few months ago, we started talking clothes, and it wasn't long until we came up with our own company: KV Fashions.

Lately, we'd been stocking material so we could sew tops for a runway show we were holding at Abraham Lincoln Middle School. It hadn't been easy to get approval to use the stage, but luckily, Katie's parents were good friends with the principal, and we'd promised all the money from ticket sales would go to improving the campus. Plus, Katie pointed out that our success could also be good for the school.

That was, of course, before the Great Crimson Crisis.

"The fabric company ran out of our color and thought we'd settle for this!" Katie threw the swatch down in disgust, and it landed on top of Tim's mac 'n' cheese. He calmly used it to wipe the corner of his mouth and then kept eating.

"Maybe you can find the red you want at a fabric store in town," suggested Heather.

I shook my head. "We already looked. The closest match Dee's Fabric World had was cherry, which was a little dark, and ketchup, which was a little ugly."

Heather and Brooke laughed.

I shrugged at Katie. "We're just gonna have to make the poppy work. Who knows? Maybe it'll look better than the crimson."

Katie leaned over and put a hand on mine. "You are so brave, Vanny."

Tim nudged Brooke. "Did the meaning of that word change while I was in the lunch line?"

"I wouldn't say 'brave,'" I told Katie while I pinched Tim's arm. "Just optimistic."

She nodded and stood, pulling her phone out of her back pocket. "Excuse me. I have to call my mom, my dad, and my life coach."

"I can't believe you guys are still waiting for fabric to come in," said Brooke as Katie hurried away. "If I were you—"

"You wouldn't be wearing sweatpants right now?" I asked with an innocent smile.

Brooke lifted one of her legs. "These are comfy *and* functional, which is exactly what I told Abel when he called me Lazy McSweatpants this morning." She lowered her leg and narrowed her eyes. "Did he tell you to mock them?"

Abel Hart was her seventh-grade boyfriend who loved to tease her almost as much as I did. Brooke would've worn gym shorts to the school dance if that was an option.

"Abel didn't need to tell me. Those things demand to be judged," I said.

Brooke stuck her tongue out at me. "What I was *going* to say was that if I were you, I would've already had all the clothes sewn and on hangers by now."

"Ha!" said Tim. "This from the girl who's usually the last to turn in her assignment for the paper?"

Brooke, Heather, Tim, and I write an advice column, "Lincoln's Letters," for our school's newspaper, the *Lincoln Log*. And despite the fact that Brooke is our section leader, she definitely doesn't set the best example.

Brooke raised her eyebrow and countered, "This from the guy who's usually the last to show up for class?"

Heather waved the scrap of cloth between them. "Break it up, you two! Truce!"

"Technically, a red flag is a symbol for battle," said Tim, "so you're actually telling us to go for it. Unless you're color-blind and think that's white." He gestured at the fabric.

Heather narrowed her eyes in mock disapproval. "Do you want to see even more red? Because I can make that happen."

"Ooh!" said Brooke and I.

Tim grinned and leaned back, holding up his hands. "Okay, okay! I've never seen your dark side before, and I'm kind of scared of it."

I laughed. "Does Heather even *have* a dark side?"

Brooke leaned forward and spoke in a whisper. "I'll bet it involves texting in all caps. And *not* saying thank you!"

The rest of us laughed, including Heather. Of our group, she was the most level-headed person and more likely to stop a fight than start one.

"Hey, I can be tough when I need to be," she assured us. "Just tell me I can only have one serving at an all-you-can-eat buffet and watch the meat loaf fly."

"Flying meat loaf." Brooke shuddered. "That stuff's scary enough when it's just sitting on a plate."

We all laughed again.

"Anyway, to get back to what you were saying earlier," I told Brooke, "I'll have you know it takes me two days to make a top *with* embellishments.

I only need seven for this show, and I've already made three. I still have plenty of time to find my models, sew the rest of my shirts, and have the fittings."

"Pfft. Models," Brooke scoffed. "So lame."

"Really? I was hoping you'd be one."

"I'd love to!" she beamed, and I rolled my eyes.

"As long as what I wear is dignified," she added.

"Too late," I said. "You're wearing a donkey costume with Tim."

"Dibs on the front end!" he said.

I turned to Heather. "I know you're not a huge fan of being singled out, but would you consider at least wearing one look down the runway? For me?" I pressed my hands together and gave her a pleading pout.

Heather smiled. "If it's for you, I think I can make an exception."

I reached over and squeezed her. "Yay!"

"Do you need help finding the rest of the models?" asked Tim. "Because I would be willing to sacrifice my time for the search." He put on his most solemn expression.

I narrowed my eyes. "If I didn't know you so well, I'd *almost* think you were offering to help me and not yourself."

"It's been a slow winter in the dating world," he confessed.

"Has it been a slow winter?" Brooke tilted her head. "Or have girls finally written enough bad things about you in Locker 411?"

"Ooh!" Heather and I said.

Tim pointed at Brooke. "That is also entirely possible."

Locker 411 was something Tim's twin sister, Gabby, created as an info source for all students. Kids can post in the different topic binders with gossip and announcements.

"Speaking of which," I said, "that's actually

where we put our sign-up sheet for our model search. It's really been filling up." I beamed. "We've got about fifteen people to choose from so far."

"And we're about to have more!" Katie rushed back toward the table, this time in striped socks, with her phone and boots in hand. "You'll never guess what my mom just told me!"

"Running in heels is a bad idea?" asked Brooke.

Katie hesitated. "You'll never guess what *else* my mom just told me!" Instead of waiting for more guesses, she plowed ahead. "My dad knows a buyer at a local boutique, and she's going to sit in on our fashion show. If she likes what she sees, our designs could be on the rack by summer!"

Instantly, I was out of my seat. "Are you serious?"

Katie nodded. "Serious as the pain shooting up my legs!"

I squealed and hugged her, bouncing up and down. She squealed, too, but followed it with, "Vanny, you're jumping on my foot!"

"Sorry, I'm just so excited!" I backed away and clutched my hands to my chest. "We could be in a *boutique*!" I turned to my other friends, and they smiled.

"That's awesome!" agreed Brooke.

"So proud of you!" said Heather.

"Very cool. Which store?" asked Tim.

"Lazenby's," said Katie.

"Ooh! I love that place," said Heather. "And now I love it even more!"

"Lazenby's?" I asked. "Wow, I haven't shopped there in ages."

It was in an older shopping center near the edge of town, which made it too far to go alone. And if Mom had to drive, I'd rather she take me into Chicago where there were loads more options.

"Hey, money is money," said Tim. "If you don't want it, I'll take it."

He's been on a get-rich-quick kick since he became best friends with Berkeley Dennis, whose parents are billionaires or something.

Tim did have a point, though. I glanced up at the cafeteria clock and faced Katie. "We have fifteen minutes before I have to get to Journalism. I think it's time to pay a visit to Locker 411 and fix our flyer. Shall we?"

"We shall!" Katie made a sweeping gesture down the hall. "But walk ahead of me, because I have to put my boots back on, and I may need you to break my fall if I stumble."

"Heh. That's the first time I've heard someone else say that and not me," I commented.

I waved to the rest of my friends and walked with Katie to Locker 411. Along with binders of info, the inner walls of the locker were lined with notes about upcoming fund-raisers and the latest gossip. Our model audition sign-up sheet had been taped on the inside of the door. At first, I'd been worried people would doodle all over the stock photos of models that decorated the sheet, but so far only one of the pictures had a mustache.

"Should we take this down and put up a new flyer or—"

I stopped as something taped beside our ad caught my eye.

It was a clipping from the previous week's advice column of a question from an anonymous reader who went by the name Wigging Out.

Dear Lincoln's Letters,

My hair is really thin, so I've been pretty much bald my whole life. And I'm a girl. This means I wear a wig to school. Nobody's figured out that it's not my real hair yet, but I'm getting tired of the same style and color. Do you think anyone would notice if I changed wigs?

Since I was in charge of giving fashion and beauty advice for the column, I'd answered the question, but someone had scribbled over my words with a black marker:

Who is Wigging Out? Put your guess below.

People were trying to figure out who this poor girl without any hair was?

Beneath that were two names, the top one scribbled in pencil and the other in blue ink.

The one in pencil said *Katie Kestler.*

My jaw dropped.

"Vanny?" Katie nudged me. "You okay?"

Before I could block the clipping, she glanced past me and laughed.

"Wow. Someone thinks I wear a wig? I've got

to start brushing my hair more."

"Is it true?" I asked before I could stop the words from coming out.

Katie grinned and tugged hard on a section of her hair. "What do you think?"

"I think we should get rid of this." I reached up and tore down the column clipping, along with our flyer.

"Who do you suppose Wigging Out *is*?" asked Katie.

"It doesn't matter," I said, crumpling up both papers. "She was someone who needed help, and that's all anyone needs to know."

The bell rang to end first lunch. Instantly, the noise level and crowds in the hall increased as everyone tried to make good use of the ten minutes before the second half of the school day.

"I'll work on our flyer and post a new one after Journalism." I raised my voice above the noise, and Katie nodded.

"Don't forget to mention the Lazenby's rep!"

I grinned. "How could I?" I gestured around us. "By summertime, all these kids are gonna be wearing KV Fashions!"

Katie and I high-fived, and she squeezed her way between two seventh graders to escape. One of them, a cute guy with dimples and shaggy hair, looked up and grinned when he saw me.

I was lucky to call that guy, Gil Pendleton, my boyfriend.

"Hi!" I said when he came over.

"I'm so excited to see you!" he said, hugging me.

I laughed. "You're gonna see me in Journalism in a few minutes!"

Gil wrote the horoscopes for the *Lincoln Log* and was also its secondary photographer.

"I know, but I wanted to share some ideas I had for filming the fashion show." He glanced at the crumpled flyer in one of my hands and the crumpled advice column in the other. "You know, if you want to make snowballs, there's actual snow outside."

I smirked. "One of these is our fashion show flyer. Someone thought it would be fun to doodle on it."

He rubbed his chin. "Mustache-wearing model?"

"How'd you guess?" I marveled.

Gil beamed. "Typical portrait graffiti. My other guess was going to be devil horns."

"Maybe that'll happen on the next one," I said with a giggle. "But first I have to add a note that we're going to have a special guest in the audience at the fashion show." I paused for dramatic effect. "A buyer from Lazenby's boutique!"

"Score!" Gil held up his hand, and I high-two'ed it since I was still holding the papers in both hands.

I tossed the flyer and clipping into the garbage and said, "That other one was from some mean kid who was trying to get people to guess who wears a wig in this school. I ripped it down before anyone else could guess."

"One of the many reasons I think you're great," he said with a smile.

As we headed to class together, he shared his idea for filming the fashion show.

"I don't think video is going to be the best medium," he said. "I think I'll stick with photos. And I won't snap the models while they're on the runway," he continued. "I don't want the flash of other people's cameras to take away from the clothes. After the show we can reenact the runway walks, and I'll take photos then."

"All good ideas!" I grinned up at him as we walked toward the newsroom. "And those are some of the many reasons I think *you're* great."

I was so busy looking at Gil that I didn't see Brooke in the doorway until I collided with her back. She stumbled forward, spilling a bottle of orange soda down the front of our editor, Mary Patrick's, white shirt.

Mary Patrick gasped and recoiled, holding her sopping shirt away from her.

"Sorry!" Brooke and I said at the same time.

Brooke added to Mary Patrick, "Orange is a really good color on you."

Mary Patrick glowered at her and stormed down the hall. "We are not done with this conversation!" she shouted over her shoulder to Brooke.

"What conversation?" I asked while Brooke wiped soda from her hands onto her sweatpants. I wrinkled my nose. "And how clever that those double as a napkin."

"Would you rather I use something else?" She reached toward my face with a sticky hand, and I squealed and ducked. "Mary Patrick said someone posted something from the advice column in Locker 411."

I made a face. "Yeah, I pulled it down as soon as I saw it."

Brooke wrinkled her forehead in confusion. "You couldn't have. She did it this morning."

Brooke handed over a piece of paper similar to the one I'd just ripped off the locker door. It was a different advice question, though: the first one that Tim had ever answered, from a kid we assigned the pseudonym Sir Stinks a Lot. Across Tim's answer, just like mine, someone had scribbled *Who is Sir Stinks a Lot?*, followed by several guesses people had written in.

This time I knew the answer because the kid, Riley Cobb, had signed the original letter with his real name. We'd changed it to protect his identity, but unfortunately, one of the guesses beneath the mystery question was actually right.

"When did Mary Patrick say she found this?" I asked.

"And why are some girls' names on here?" Gil asked with a chuckle.

"She said she found it right after second period," Brooke answered me. "But you noticed it in the locker just now?"

I frowned. "Not this one but another advice request that people tried to guess the secret identity to. It was posted right next to the model search flyer that Katie and I put up last week."

Brooke's eyes widened, and she held out her hand. "Let me see!"

I bit my lip. "I threw away the clipping after I tore it down."

"What?" Brooke smacked her hand to her forehead. "V, you can't destroy evidence!"

"I'll go see if I can find it," said Gil.

I smiled at him gratefully as he jogged away. Then I turned back to Brooke. "Sorry, but I didn't know it was evidence when I saw it. I just thought someone was being a jerk."

She shook her head. "Someone's doing worse than that. They're trying to make the advice column look bad." She narrowed her eyes. "And I have a feeling I know who it is."

I'd seen that hatred in Brooke's eyes before. She saved it especially for one boy who'd tried to get her removed from writing fitness advice *and* who'd blackmailed Tim into being his servant.

"Ryan Durstwich?" I asked.

"Ryan Durstwich," Brooke agreed with a nod of her auburn ponytail. "That greasy, slimy creep. I wonder where he's hiding now."

"Right behind you."

Brooke and I screamed in surprise, clutching at each other. Ryan rolled his eyes and crossed his arms.

"Let me know when you're done overreacting."

Brooke got over her surprise quicker than I did and scowled at Ryan. "What's with this?"

She took the advice column clipping Mary Patrick had found and thrust it in his face.

Ryan took a step back and studied it. "I'm not Sir Stinks a Lot."

"Could've fooled me," said Brooke. "But I'm not talking about that. Why are you trying to figure out who he is?" She tapped the question written in marker.

He raised an eyebrow. "That's actually why I'm here. Are you still part of the Lil Sherlocks club?"

From the way Brooke's anger evaporated, I could tell she hadn't been expecting *that* question.

"Uh, it's Young Sherlocks," she said. "And yeah. Why?"

Young Sherlocks was a club that Abel had created. Its members watched crime shows and movies and tried to solve cases around school.

Ryan glanced at me out of the corner of his

eye. "I have a case I want to discuss with you. Privately," he told Brooke.

It was her turn to cross her arms. "Anything you have to say, you can say in front of me *and* Vanessa."

"Yeah, I cut your hair for free once," I reminded him.

"And almost clipped off my ear," he added.

"You shouldn't have tried to run away!"

Brooke held up a hand to silence me. "Ryan, what do you need?"

He looked around and stepped closer. "If I tell you about this, you can't tell anyone else."

"Agreed," Brooke said.

After one last sidelong glance at me, he held up a piece of paper that was becoming all too familiar. An advice column question with marker scrawled over the answer.

"I want you to stop whoever's trying to expose me," said Ryan.

CHAPTER

2

The Greatest Show on Earth

Brooke and I exchanged a troubled glance.

"Okay, two notes is a strange coincidence," I said. "But three . . ."

"Is a pattern. When did you find this?" Brooke asked Ryan, reaching for the paper.

"Right before lunch," he said.

"Huh," I said. "It seems like as soon as one gets taken down, another gets put up."

"You're right!" Brooke took off at a sprint toward Locker 411, and I followed.

"Hey! Are you gonna help?" Ryan called after us.

"If you tell our teacher we'll be late for class!" I shouted back.

Ryan frowned but poked his head into the newsroom to talk to Mrs. Higginbotham (we call her Mrs. H).

"If we're lucky, we can catch whoever it is in the act," Brooke told me as we rounded the corner.

Nobody was waiting at Locker 411, but when Brooke opened the door, the space I'd left behind had been filled with another advice clipping. And someone's name had already been suggested.

"This is so weird," Brooke muttered, pulling out her cell phone. She snapped a picture of the locker and closed the door.

"You aren't going to take down the note?" I asked.

She shook her head. "Whoever put this up

will be back to check on the results. All we have to do is get out of the newsroom before the end of class and wait to see who shows up."

I nodded. "I have to come back here anyway, to put up a new flyer for the fashion show try-outs."

"Great! It'll be the perfect excuse." Brooke and I headed back toward the newsroom as the bell rang. "By the way, you never told me what I'll be wearing for that modeling thing. It's not an evening gown, is it?"

"I wouldn't put you in an evening gown," I assured her. "Your sweatpants wouldn't fit underneath."

She bumped me. "Seriously!"

"We're only showcasing tops, remember? And I have a cute, sporty one in mind that would be perfect for you."

Brooke grinned. "I hate to admit it, but I'm

actually really excited about this!"

I didn't even bother acting offended. "Me too! Especially since there's going to be a buyer in the crowd!"

We stopped at the advice box outside the newsroom so Brooke could grab the latest help requests, and smiled apologetically at Mrs. H as we took our seats. She shook her head and pointed to her watch, but I didn't feel too guilty. There was still an empty chair in the back that Tim would soon try to sneak into.

"Where have you guys been?" asked Heather. But before we could answer, she held up a finger. "Tim's coming."

She gestured to the door just as he charged in.

Mrs. H sighed. "Why do we have warning bells if you're all going to ignore them?"

"Sorry, Mrs. H!" he said.

She flipped through her roster. "Three times

in a month, Mr. Antonides. I'm afraid that's a write-up."

There was a chorus of "oooo" from around the room, and an "aww" from Tim as Mrs. H pulled out a pink slip of paper.

Brooke nudged Heather. "How did you know Tim was coming, anyway?"

"He wanted change for the snack machine, and all I had was pennies. I heard his pockets jingling down the hall," she said with a grin. Then to Tim, "I told you the machine wouldn't take them."

Tim dropped a pack of M&M's on his desk. "Luckily, a girl took pity on me after she saw me put in twenty-five pennies."

Heather rolled her eyes. "Why am I not surprised?"

Tim grinned. "You should be proud of how resourceful I am! Now I've got food *and* money."

He patted a coin-filled pocket.

"Yeah, *my* money," said Heather. "Which means I'm entitled to at least a handful of M&M's." She cupped her hand and looked at him expectantly.

Tim eyed it with suspicion. "This was your plan all along, wasn't it? To make *me* get candy for you!"

Heather revealed the tiniest smile. "You'll never know." She pointed to her palm, and Tim finally poured some M&M's into it.

"What's with the poor man's routine?" Brooke asked Tim. "I know for a fact you earn double my allowance."

"I'm saving," he said. "I've got my eyes on an expensive prize." He popped some M&M's into his mouth.

"Is it clothes?" I gasped and grabbed his arm. "Is it Thomas Pink?"

Tim almost choked on his candy but managed to ask, "Who?"

"Don't bother getting excited," Brooke told me. "Tim's probably having a painting done of himself."

"Which I'm sure the Louvre Museum would happily hang next to the *Mona Lisa*," said Tim. "But no, that's not what I'm saving for."

"Some wordy book where the characters say 'thou' and 'thine'?" Brooke guessed again.

He shook some more candy into his palm. "There's nothing wrong with the classics, but if you think they're too wordy, you can get them as graphic novels." He chewed thoughtfully. "Oh wait. You're more into pop-up books, aren't you?"

Heather and I giggled, and Brooke swiped one of Tim's M&M's. "For your information, I read at an advanced level. Just this weekend, I finished three Agatha Christie novels."

Tim raised an eyebrow. "Uh-oh. I'm pretty sure those are classics. We're gonna have to take your cool card."

"She lost that when she put these on." I reached over and popped the elastic waistband of Brooke's sweatpants.

"Why is it Pick on Brooke Day?" she asked.

Mrs. H called Tim to the front to get his pink slip, and we pounced on his M&M's as soon as he walked away.

Heather swallowed her candy and poked Brooke in the arm. "What were you saying before Penny Pants came in?" she asked, cocking her head in Tim's direction.

Brooke smiled and explained about the articles Mary Patrick and I had found. She kept her word and left Ryan out of it.

"Someone's trying to embarrass other kids? That's so mean!" said Heather. "Do you have the columns with you?"

Brooke produced the one Mary Patrick had given her, and I got Gil's attention.

"Any luck with that paper I threw away?" I asked.

"It was covered with yogurt by the time I got to it," he said, wrinkling his nose. "At least I hope it was yogurt."

Heather glanced from the clipping to us. "Who would be horrible enough to post secrets about other students?"

"Horrible? Secrets?" Tim dropped into his seat, pink paper in hand. "We must be talking about Ryan Durstwich."

Brooke shook her head. "I already confronted him, and he had a solid alibi. V and I are going to scope out the locker, though, to see if we can catch the Phantom Dirt Digger." She smiled. "You like the nickname? I'm proud of it."

There was loud clapping from the front of the room as Mrs. H called the class to attention.

"Boys and girls, we've got another award-winning issue of the *Lincoln Log* to churn out," she said with a smile. "That is, of course, if you're still interested in competing at the state level."

A few weeks back our school had entered its most recent issue of the *Lincoln Log* into a county-wide contest for school newspapers, and we won! It automatically advanced us to the state-level contest, which was going to prove even more challenging, so Mrs. H and Mary Patrick had been pushing us to come up with even better articles.

"Why don't we get the ball rolling with the front page?" she asked.

As the different sections provided their input, an idea dawned on me, and I waved my hand wildly in the air.

"Bathroom pass is on my desk," said Mrs. H.

"No, not that." I ignored the warmth in my cheeks and the giggles around the classroom.

"You know how Katie Kestler and I are having a fashion show? Well, it turns out there's going to be a buyer from Lazenby's boutique in the audience!"

Mrs. H pressed her hands together. "Vanessa, that's wonderful!"

Mary Patrick pointed a marker at Felix, the team leader for front-page news. "Can you make room for an interview with Vanessa and Katie about their show? That's winning material right there."

Felix flipped through a couple pages in his notebook. "We'll have to shift some things around, but we can make it work."

"You should also have someone report on the actual fashion show," Brooke piped up. "I mean, how often does *that* happen in middle school?"

I flashed her a grateful smile.

Mrs. H nodded. "Excellent idea! We could also include the show specifics in the interview, in order to increase attendance. Vanessa, when is the show, and how much are tickets?"

"It's next Friday, after school," I said. "And admission is two bucks a person."

"What?!" Tim spun in his chair to face me. "You're only charging two dollars?"

All eyes were on me, and I fidgeted in my seat. "Well, we thought kids might not come if they had to pay more."

"V, you're looking at this all wrong," he said. "People appreciate what they have to pay for. If you're throwing a cheap show, they aren't going to take you seriously."

"I agree with Tim!" Brooke pounded her desk with a fist. "Twenty bucks a head!"

Several kids in the class booed.

"Yeah, that's a little high," said Tim. "But you should at least be charging five dollars a person."

I gave him a dubious look. "You think?"

He nodded. "Maybe ten if you add a VIP section with swag bags."

That got my interest.

"VIP," I whispered. The initials practically sparkled before my eyes.

Katie and I had been thinking too small. Of course we needed a VIP section! We were KV Fashions!

"What would be in the swag bags?" asked Heather.

I turned to Tim, and he smiled craftily.

"I'll make you a deal. I'll take care of marketing and event planning for your show if you give me profits from any VIP upgrades I sell."

"But all the money we make has to go to the school," I said with a frown.

"For general admission," he pointed out. "The VIP experience is an added level."

I nodded slowly. "Let me talk it over with Katie and Principal Winslow. We don't want the cost to keep kids away either."

Mary Patrick cleared her throat. "If I can interrupt, the only person you really need there is the buyer, correct? She's the one you have to impress."

"True," I said.

"I mean, it'll be great if kids like your clothes, but if Lazenby's doesn't like them, that's a big problem."

"Who wouldn't fall in love with V's fashions?" asked Heather, shooting me a confident smile.

I smiled back, but it wasn't as confident.

I'd been so excited about the idea of a buyer at the show, I hadn't even considered whether she'd like my fashions. What if she didn't?

"Then it's settled," said Tim. "Vanessa and Katie will charge five dollars for general admission and ten dollars for a VIP upgrade." He nodded to Felix. "Make sure that's in the article."

Mrs. H looked to me. "Are you okay with that, Vanessa?"

"Yeah," I said, "as long as Principal Winslow and Katie are."

She nodded. "Double-check and let us know as soon as possible." Mrs. H moved on to the next piece, and shortly after, we broke into our section groups.

"Look, I know you're not crazy about the idea of charging more," Tim said to me. "But if you ever want to make money, you have to start somewhere."

"Plus, you have to pay for all that fabric," added Brooke.

"Not really. Katie gets it at a huge discount," I said. Her father worked at a textile company.

"A discount means you're still paying," said Tim.

"Fine," I said. "We've already decided what to charge for admission, so let's move past that.

I need to make sure the Lazenby's buyer is impressed."

"What do you mean?" asked Heather. "That's what your clothes are for."

"Right, but I have to make sure the buyer loves them. Word gets around in the biz."

Brooke raised an eyebrow. "'The biz'? You're not bringing Van Jackson back, are you?"

Heather elbowed her. "Why would you even mention that?" she whispered loudly. "Van Jackson is trouble!"

Van Jackson was an alter ego I'd used a couple times to showcase my designer side. For some reason my friends weren't fans. Probably because Van Jackson was bossy and a bit of a diva. But she made me feel confident.

"You're taking way too long to say no," said Tim, watching me nervously.

I rolled my eyes. "I'm not bringing Van Jackson back."

All three of my friends breathed sighs of relief.

"But like I said, I need to make sure I can impress the buyer," I told them. "Give her what she wants."

Brooke gave me a dubious look. "Can you read minds? Because that's the only way you'll know."

Tim held up a finger. "Actually, V could scout out the store. It's what my parents do when they're checking on the competition." Tim's parents owned a few small grocery stores in town.

Brooke smiled. "What's there to compete for in their business? Who has the tallest stack of soda cans?"

"Lots of stuff! Prices, products, and yes, presentation." Tim counted them off.

I tapped my fingertips on the desk. "You know, that's not a bad idea. I should go to Lazenby's and see what they carry."

"How about today?" asked Heather. "My grandma is picking me up, but we can ask her to take a side trip. She loves Lazenby's, too."

"Great!" I said. "Brooke, you wanna come?"

She made a face. "I can't. Lacey and I are doing some one-on-one training with the girls on the team."

Brooke was captain of her traveling soccer team, the Berryville Strikers, and Lacey Black was her cocaptain.

"They're still not looking great?" asked Heather.

Brooke shrugged. "They're coming along, but we decided to cross-train a couple more girls in case we lose another starter like we did last month." She produced the advice requests she'd taken from the box. "But enough about our personal lives. Let's help some strangers with theirs!"

Five minutes before the end of class, Brooke bumped my arm.

"Ready to try and confront the Phantom?"

I picked up my new flyer. "I want to, but I should really talk to Katie between classes. Especially about these new changes."

Brooke plucked the paper from my hand. "Then I'll take care of this for you *and* stake out the Phantom on my own."

"I can help," said Heather. "I even have the perfect cover. There's a water fountain across from Locker 411. We can take turns drinking and watching."

"You're hired!" Brooke passed her the flyer. "Let's go ask Mrs. H if we can leave early."

"I hope they catch whoever it is," I told Tim when Brooke and Heather left.

He nodded. "How do you feel about hors d'oeuvres?"

I blinked at him. "Huh?"

"Before the fashion show. Or after. It's your call."

"Why does there need to be food at all?" I

asked. "That's just going to cost more money, isn't it?"

"Not necessarily. I had a brilliant idea." He tapped his head with an index finger. "What if your fashion show had sponsors?"

I gasped and grabbed his arm. "That would be so professional! Yes, please, oh my gosh, let's do that," I babbled.

Tim laughed. "I'm on it."

As soon as the bell rang to end Journalism, I dashed down the hall to Katie's class.

"Guess what, guess what, guess what?" I gripped her arms and shook them.

"You just drank five sodas?" she asked.

"No! Our fashion show is going to be the talk of the town!" I told her about Tim's suggestions, and by the time I was done, she was even more excited than I was.

"First a buyer, now a VIP section. We are so legit! Seriously, if Kate Spade called just to chat,

I wouldn't be surprised." She paused. "Okay, maybe a little bit."

I chuckled. "Heather and I are going to Lazenby's after school to see what they carry. You know, to get an idea of what they're looking for. Can you come?"

Katie's expression turned pained. "Mega bummer! I'm going with my mom to sort out the fabric mess. But if you see something cute, buy two!"

"So I can make you twice as jealous?" I asked with a grin.

Katie giggled and hugged herself. "Just think of it, Vanny. Our designs at Lazenby's!"

But when Heather and I walked into the store later that afternoon, all I could think of was turning around and walking back out. The air smelled musty and felt damp, and the clothing on display by the entrance made me wonder if Lazenby's shoppers got beat up on a regular basis. Lots of pastels, floral prints, polka dots . . . everything babyish that I'd given up when I learned how to tie my shoes.

Heather gestured to all the clothes with a flourish. "Ta-da! Do you like them?"

I liked that I wasn't *wearing* them.

"They've certainly come up with a lot of uses for yarn" was all I said. "I would've never thought to knit a vest." I squinted at it. "Or decorate it with butterflies."

Heather gasped. "V, look at how cute!" She rushed to a clothing rack and pointed to a sweater set and plaid skirt. "I could pair this with my fake pearls."

And then be mistaken for someone's grandma, I said to myself.

"Sure," I said aloud. "That would be nice." I pushed items along the rack and studied them. "In fact, it's probably your best option."

Heather tilted her head to one side. "V, I successfully combined clothing *and* accessories.

Normally, you'd proudly carry me across the room on your shoulders."

"And then I'd drop you because I'm clumsy," I said with a nod.

Heather giggled. "Then what's wrong? I figured you'd be gushing over all this stuff."

"Close," I said, "if you change the word 'gushing' to 'throwing up.'"

Her eyes widened. "What? You really think they're that bad?"

She looked so personally offended that I reached for her arm. "Sorry; they're fine. Just not my style. I prefer something with a bit more sass, you know? Something edgy and daring."

A saleswoman walked over, clad in a sweater set of her own, with shoulder pads that could've doubled as pillows. "Hello, girls! Are we looking for something special?"

"We're looking for something edgy and daring," said Heather.

The saleswoman took in Heather's outfit: green henley, denim skirt, and tights. Then she took in *my* outfit: purple leggings, striped knee socks, and a charcoal tunic.

"*You're* looking for something edgy?" she asked Heather.

Heather frowned and crossed her arms. "You say that like it's hard to believe, but I'm pretty tough. As we speak, my grandma is ordering me extra-spicy Szechuan food in the restaurant two doors down."

The saleswoman smiled. "Very well. And what do you consider daring?"

Heather thought for a moment. "Asking a boy out, red lipstick, and jumping out of an airplane."

The saleswoman nodded slowly. "I meant in fashion."

"Oh!" Heather turned to me. "What do we consider daring?"

"You know, sharp angles, bright colors, buckles and zippers for decoration," I said.

"Right!" Heather pointed at me. "All of that."

The woman shook her head. "I'm sorry, but we don't carry much of that here. Lazenby's is refined and classic." She gestured to Heather as she said this.

I frowned. "But refined and classic isn't my style."

The saleswoman smiled. "Well, there *are* other stores in the complex, dear."

Lazenby's was refined, classic, *and* snobby. I was starting to wonder why I even cared to impress its buyer.

"Just out of curiosity, how much does this store sell a month?" I asked.

The saleswoman arced a brow. "We do well enough that we're signing millionaire-model Trinity Fawn to our next ad campaign."

"Trinity Fawn?" I squeaked. Having her wear the clothes I made would be a dream come true!

Someone else came in through the entrance, and the saleswoman smiled at us once more. "If you'd like to try something on, just let me know." She walked off to help the new customer who definitely looked more like she belonged there.

I turned to Heather. "I *have* to have Trinity Fawn in my fashions."

Heather wrinkled her forehead. "Vanessa, you heard the lady. They don't carry your style here."

"Then I'll just have to come up with a style they do carry," I said with an emphatic nod. I pulled out my cell phone and brought up the camera.

"But I thought you hated this stuff," said Heather. "What are you doing?"

"Getting some design ideas," I said, snapping a few pictures of the clothes around me. "You've got to give the people what they want, right?"

Heather frowned. "V, you're not gonna . . ."

"I'm totally gonna," I said with a firm nod. "My fashions aren't what they're looking for, so it's back to the drawing board."

CHAPTER 3

In the Name of Fashion

Even my photo printer seemed to hate the outfits at Lazenby's. With every image, it gurgled and whined as I printed out what I'd seen in the store.

"Sorry," I told it as I picked up the latest photo it spat out. "I feel your pain."

I tacked the photo to the corkboard wall of my bedroom, along with others I'd placed in the shape of a frownie face.

There was a knock at my door, which was thrown open a second later. My brother, Terrell, never knocks and my mom always waits for me to answer, which meant it could only be one person.

"Hey, Katie," I said, not taking my eyes off the wall.

"Vanny, things are really happening!" She paused when she saw the pinned-up photos. "Aw. Why is your wall so sad?" She stepped closer to study the photos. "And why are those clothes so *Titanic*?"

Now I looked at her. "*Titanic*?"

She nodded. "Huge disaster that men, women, and children want to get away from."

I tapped the wall. "This is the current stock at Lazenby's. And these are the best of the bunch."

"Yeesh." Katie made a face. "We are gonna seriously have to wow the polka dots off their socks."

"That's what I'm thinking," I said. "Especially if we want to work with, oh, Trinity Fawn."

I got exactly the reaction I was expecting

from Katie, and then some.

She gasped. "Trin . . . Trin . . . You . . ." She pointed at me. "You got us a chance to work with Trinity Fawn?"

I waggled my hand from side to side. "She's going to be the new model for Lazenby's, so if they carry our line, chances are she could be wearing our tops."

Katie finally breathed and steadied herself on my desk chair.

"That's why I'm working on some new designs that'll be more their style," I said. "What have you been up to?"

In an instant, Katie's energy was back up to a thousand. She gripped my arms. "Vanny, we have the crimson fabric. And it is *so* red. Like raw beef red. At least, I'm assuming. I don't eat cow."

"Great!" I said. "Although, after seeing what Lazenby's has, I'm not sure it's right."

"And Tim and I came up with some swag for

our VIP bags!" She ignored my comment and reached into her purse, producing a shiny purple bag about the size of a deck of cards.

I smiled at it. "Are we giving away doll clothes?"

Katie shook her head and thrust the bag at me. "We, my friend, are warming some legs."

I reached into the bag and pulled out a pair of knee-high stockings. "I'll be honest—I was expecting something more glamour and less grandma."

"Don't worry. They'll actually be leg warmers. I just used these as an example." Katie took them from me and unrolled them. There were little heart stickers randomly attached to the legs. "Pretty neat, huh?"

I gave her a concerned look. "Are we looking at the same thing? Paper hearts stuck to old lady stockings?"

Katie rolled her eyes. "You're looking, but

you're not *seeing*." She held one of the nylon legs inches from my face.

"I really hope these are clean," I said.

"Look at the heart!" She jabbed at it. "See the letters inside?"

"KV," I read. Then I grinned. "That's us!"

She smiled happily. "My dad is making some custom fabric with our logo on it that we can sew into leg warmers. It's cheap, it's stretchy—one size fits all!"

"It's perfect!" I said. "Although I'm not crazy about the heart logo."

Katie held up a finger. "I thought you might feel that way." She reached into her purse again. "Which is why I came up with these!" She pulled out a sheet of scribblings.

"What else do you have in there?" I asked, peering into her purse. "A sewing machine?"

She shook the designs at me. "Vanny! We

don't have much time! The design has to be turned in tonight."

"AHH! Why didn't you say so?" I settled onto the carpet and spread the scribblings in front of me, casting my vote for each. "No, no, maybe. A unicorn?" I looked up at Katie, and she shrugged.

"They're special and magical, just like our fashions."

I shook my head. "We want to look like professionals. This logo has to last for the rest of our lives."

"The rest of our lives!" Katie dropped down and hugged me. "Oh, Vanny. I would love to be business partners forever. When we're old, we can design sweaters for the other old people we play cards with!"

I laughed and hugged her back. "Well, let's start with a logo. I like having our initials in it, so people remember it's us and not just, say, a unicorn." I made a face, and she pushed me.

"Me too," she said.

I studied all the different versions of *KV*, which were scrawled on every square inch of the page, even on the side of the page and upside down. I tilted my head to different angles.

"You ever notice how much alike a K and a V look?" I asked. "If we combine them, you get this."

I grabbed a sketch pad and pencil from my desk and drew what I was thinking of:

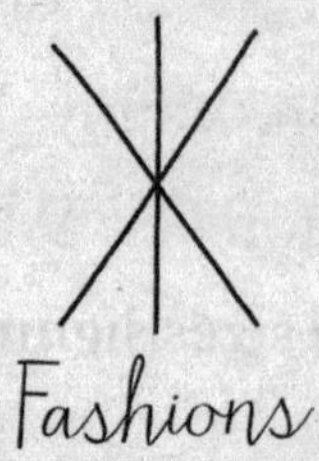

Katie gasped and picked up the sketch pad. "Vanny, this is perfect! It looks like a star—which is what we are!"

"And it would look really cute on leg

warmers," I said. "We'd just leave off the wording."

She took a picture of the sketch. "I'm going to send this to my dad. He can have one of his designers clean it up a bit, and then we'll have our very own fabric."

My disappointment with the Lazenby's visit was rapidly being replaced by excitement. "This is going to be so cool! I'm so glad Tim thought of swag bags."

Katie nodded. "He was really helpful when I was trying to recruit models earlier, too."

I rolled my eyes. "Oh, I'm sure he was helping himself just as much as you."

"No, no, no!" She waved her hands. "He had girls of all looks and sizes signing up! And I think Brooke was interested, too," Katie said with a smile. "She kept watching us while she pretended to drink from the water fountain."

I grinned. "I think she was on a stakeout, actually. Trying to catch whoever posted that advice clipping, and a few others. I'm surprised she didn't chase you away."

Katie smacked her forehead. "That's why she came over and started coughing on everyone! I got a little worried when she said something about the plague."

I nodded. "That's how she gets us to the front of the line for crowded movies, too."

My phone rang, and I leaned over and saw Tim's name. "Speaking of crazy friends." I picked it up and answered, "Please do not ask what kind of hors d'oeuvres I want at the show."

"Hello to you, too!" said Tim. "And I wasn't calling to ask about food. I was calling about the music."

"Music?" I repeated.

Tim chuckled. "Oh, V. You can't have models walking the runway in silence!"

"Oh, Tim. We're not," I replied. "We're hooking my cell phone to a speaker and playing music."

Katie stooped low and shouted into the phone. "I've been working on the playlist!"

Tim made a scoffing sound. "Amateur hour."

"We *are* amateurs," I reminded him. "What would *you* suggest?"

"Are you ready to have your mind blown? I'm thinking . . . ," He paused for effect. "A DJ."

I sighed. "What? No DJ, crazy."

"Oh, no. DJ Crazy is way too expensive," said Tim. "I was thinking of someone more up-and-coming. A guy you might have seen around school."

Katie poked me in the arm. "What's going on?"

"Tim wants to DJ at the show," I said.

"Not me," said Tim. "I don't have that kind of talent. But Lil Chill—"

"His name is Lil Chill?" I interrupted.

"His beats are very ill," said Tim. "And he has all his own equipment."

I rolled my eyes. "Gee, I wonder who you

know who could afford something like that."

"Berkeley seriously wants to get into the music business," continued Tim, "and he played me one of his sample tracks. It's really good!"

I muted the phone and spoke to Katie, who'd been poking my leg. "Berkeley Dennis wants to DJ our fashion show."

Her eyes lit up. "Awesome!"

I sighed. "I was afraid you'd say that."

"Hello? V?" Tim spoke into my ear.

I unmuted the phone. "We have runway auditions tomorrow. Berkeley can play during that, and if he does a good job, he can do the live show."

Tim cheered. "You rock, V!"

"*Berkeley* better rock," I told him. "Was there anything else you wanted to talk about? Like offering free helicopter rides or having the models ride in on horses?"

Tim hesitated. "Are either of those actual possibilities?"

"Good-bye, Tim." I ended the call and looked at Katie. "So now we've got a VIP section, swag bags, and a DJ." I tried my best to sound annoyed, but as I listed off each item, I actually found the corners of my mouth curving up. We were turning into kind of a big deal!

Katie was smiling, too. "This is how it starts, Vanny! Today, Berryville. Tomorrow, the world!" She gestured to my photo wall. "We've already got a store interested in us."

My smile thinned out. "But do we? Look at what they like." I pointed to the images. "And look at what I like." I gestured to my outfit.

There was another knock on my door, followed by silence.

"Come in, Mom!" I said.

She opened the door and then smiled at us. "Vanessa, honey, dinner's ready. Katie, you're welcome to stay."

We both got to our feet, and Katie picked up

her purse. "Thanks, Mrs. Jackson, but I should probably be getting home. Bobbi's making TLTs tonight."

"Your mom's making *what*?" I asked.

"Tofu, lettuce, and tomato sandwiches," said Katie.

I did my best not to throw up on her shoes because it would've been rude *and* because her shoes were really cute.

Katie let herself out, and I followed Mom to the kitchen, where Terrell was trying to make his own sloppy joe. So far he'd managed to cover every inch of the plate and completely miss the hamburger bun.

"We're gonna have to rename these things sloppy Terrells," I told him, taking the spoon and getting ready to pour sauce over his bun. He pushed my hand away.

"I did it on purpose," he informed me. "I don't like when the bread gets soggy."

I shrugged and poured the meat sauce on my own hamburger bun. "Everyone's got their own way, I guess."

"So did you make any progress on those Lazenby's designs?" asked Mom, putting a cob of corn on Terrell's plate.

I groaned and shook my head. "I don't get the appeal of their clothes. They're so boring and tame. If you sewed live scorpions in the sleeves, I still wouldn't wear them."

Mom chuckled. "Well, that's an image."

"That would be cool!" added Terrell. He raised his arms, as if he had scorpions in the sleeves, and glared at an invisible enemy.

"You know, maybe you shouldn't try looking at this from a designer's perspective," said Mom. "Sometimes when I'm trying to identify with a tough client, I put myself in their shoes."

I wrinkled my nose. "I've seen the shoes at Lazenby's. I don't want to."

"Very funny," she said, nudging me toward the table. "You know what I mean. Don't look for what's wrong. Look for what's right."

"I did that earlier," I told her. "The result was very depressing."

She took a bite of her sloppy joe. "You said Heather liked the clothes, right? And you like Heather, right? Try to identify with her."

I snapped my fingers. "I've got a better idea!"

Mom shot me a warning look. "If you're thinking of bringing back Van Jackson, stop."

"No! Why does everyone think that?" I rolled my eyes. "You know how sometimes actors will take up their character's hobbies or eat like their character to really get into the role?"

Mom nodded. "Method acting, sure."

"I'm going to try method designing," I said. "You said put myself in Lazenby's shoes, but I'm going to put myself in their clothes. I'll bet Heather has plenty."

After dinner, I went to my room to text her, but as soon as I settled on my bed, my phone buzzed with a call from Brooke.

"Hey, how was soccer practice?" I asked.

"Not bad. We're working on channeling our anger into kicking the ball, and not each other, when we're upset."

I smiled. "And how was your stakeout?"

Brooke made a disgusted sound. "Lame. I almost drowned."

I sat up straight. "What?! Katie didn't tell me that part."

"Yeah, I was playing it cool, you know? Drinking from the water fountain while I waited for the Phantom Dirt Digger to show. For five minutes straight. I must've drunk, like, two gallons and that can't be good, considering I'm already sixty percent water."

I giggled and relaxed. "You know you could've just *pretended* to drink the water."

"Then someone might have gotten suspicious!"

I didn't bother telling her about Katie's observation. "So the culprit never showed, huh?"

"Nope. But that's not why I called. Did you happen to take all the advice requests out of the box after school?"

"After school?" I frowned. "No, Heather and I went straight to Lazenby's. Why?"

"When I went to check before I left, it was completely empty. That hasn't happened since we first started."

"Maybe Heather picked them up before we met," I said. "I need to talk to her about something, anyway, so I'll ask."

"Yeah, let me know what she says," said Brooke. "I've got to call Abel and tell him the stakeout was a bust. Maybe he and I can come up with a new plan."

"Well, hopefully, we won't have to," I told

her. "This could all be over tomorrow."

Brooke's voice took on a stiff tone and did her best Sherlock Holmes impersonation. "On the contrary, my good Vanessa, I think it's just beginning."

I shook my head and hung up with her to call Heather. When Heather answered and I told her about dressing like a Lazenby's fan, she was more than happy to help.

"I'll pack an extra outfit to bring to school," she said. "I'm so flattered you want to borrow my clothes!"

"Yeah, I really want to understand their appeal," I said.

There was silence. "Okay, now I'm slightly less flattered."

"Oh, you know what I mean! Those clothes aren't me, but I want to like them for the buyer. Help me embrace polyester!"

Heather laughed. "V, the buyer's either going

to like your designs or she's not."

"Yes, but I can make sure she does," I said, "if I know the style inside and out."

Heather sighed. "Fine. But I'm bringing the outfit I like least so that when you insult it, I won't feel so bad."

"I won't insult it," I said, crossing my fingers over my heart, even though she couldn't see me. "Also, Brooke wanted me to ask if you emptied out the advice box at the end of the day. She didn't see any requests in there after school."

Heather made a sound of surprise. "Huh. None?"

I shrugged. "That's what Brooke said. Why?"

"It might be nothing, but I haven't gotten any requests through our email account, either," she said.

"Maybe the school's email system is down," I said.

"I wondered the same thing, so I sent an email

to the address, and it came through fine. People just aren't sending advice requests."

I tapped my chin. "Weird. I'll let her know. And thanks again for the clothes!"

"Happy to help," she said. "See you tomorrow!"

When we hung up, I sent a text to Brooke telling her what Heather had said. Her response was just one word.

Uh-oh.

CHAPTER 4

Vanilla Vanessa

"Maybe we're making a big deal out of nothing," I said from beneath an unsettling amount of polyester. It was the next morning, and I was in the girls' bathroom at school, changing into the clothes Heather had brought for me. The jeans weren't too bad if I ignored the hearts sewn onto the back pockets (which I thankfully couldn't see without a mirror), but the camisole-and-sweater combo were taking some effort to love.

"Maybe we are," agreed Heather. "But, V, with Valentine's Day so close, the in-box should be flooded. All I've gotten is one letter from a girl sending flowers to herself who wants to know if adding chocolates would be too much." She paused. "How's it going in there?"

I stepped out of the stall and threw my arms in the air. "Ta-da!" I mimicked her exclamation from the day before.

Since they were Heather's clothes, I expected her to beam with pride. Instead, she tilted her head to one side.

"Huh." Then she smiled. "Well, at least they fit."

"Do I look that bad?" I asked, checking out my reflection. "Oh."

My normal clothes were bright and flashy, like a peacock, but these clothes were dull and bland, like a pigeon . . . wearing these clothes.

"It's just not you," said Heather. Then she wrinkled her nose. "Very not you. I guess they'll take some getting used to. But that's the point, right? To get the feel for this look?"

I nodded. "You're right. I want the Lazenby's buyer to see that I understand their style."

Heather smiled again. "So let's button that cardigan and hit the halls!"

"Yeah!" I said, trying to mirror her enthusiasm.

As we walked, several kids stopped and did double takes.

"Is that Vanessa Jackson?" one of them asked. "Since when does she wear sweater sets?"

"Maybe she lost a bet," someone said.

Either Heather didn't hear them or she chose to ignore them.

"Where should we stop first?" she asked. "The advice box or Locker 411?"

"Let's start with the advice box since it's closer."

But Brooke had already beaten us there. She was leaning against the wall beside the advice box and chatting up people who passed.

"Nice morning, huh? A perfect morning to get some advice! Hey, kid, you know what goes great with that breakfast burrito? A side of advice."

Heather and I approached her.

"What are you doing?" I asked at the same moment Brooke asked, "What are you wearing? You look like you work at a potpourri store."

"Hey!" said Heather. "V's in my clothes!"

"Oh." Brooke laughed nervously. "Have I mentioned how much I love potpourri? Yay, wood chips!"

Heather didn't look soothed by that response. "You guys are getting really close to hurting my feelings. I might not dress bold like Vanessa, but I definitely dress better than a lot of kids at this school and definitely better than Lazy McSweatpants." She gave Brooke a pointed look.

"I'm not wearing sweatpants today!" Brooke lifted a leg so we could see her jeans. "Mainly because my mom hid them all, but also because I know they don't look good."

Heather continued to stare at her until Brooke sighed. "I'm sorry I insulted your clothes. They look cute on you. Just not on Vanessa."

"Thanks," I said. "With tact like that, maybe you're the reason the advice box is empty." I lifted the lid. "At least, I'm assuming it's empty since you're standing out here, begging for requests."

Brooke's expression turned serious. "Guys, this is bad. If we stop getting requests, we won't have anything to submit for the state contest. And you know Mary Patrick won't like that."

Heather swallowed. "There won't be enough chocolate in the world to make her happy."

"Well, Heather and I will go check out Locker 411 and tear down any new advice clippings," I said. "But you can't stand out here. Otherwise, Mary Patrick is going to know something's up. We need to solve this without her knowing."

Heather and Brooke nodded.

"Let's go," I told Heather.

"Okay, but if you're wanting to feel like a Lazenby's customer, you need to start moving like one," she informed me as we walked. "You're still strutting like you're a supermodel in heels. You need to be stepping lighter and moving your body less."

I changed my pace. "How's that?"

Heather giggled. "You look like a robot on Slinkys."

I bounced a little less and flexed my knees a little more. "Now?"

In answer, Heather grabbed my shoulders and stepped in front of me. "Watch how I walk."

She spun around and demonstrated. "Now you try!" she called from down the hall.

I mirrored her steps, trying to think Heather-ish thoughts, like glitter-covered ponies and kittens with balls of string.

"Okay, now you're skipping. Stop skipping," she said.

"I can't help it! It's what happens when I think of kittens and ponies," I said, catching up to her.

"Kittens and ponies?" she repeated.

I nodded. "Like what you think about."

Heather laughed. "I never think of those things. Try choir and your friends."

I smiled. "You think about us when you're walking down the hall?"

"Of course! You're my best friends and some of my happiest thoughts."

I threw my arms around Heather before stepping back. "Okay, I can do this."

I tried one last time and Heather clapped. "Perfect!"

"Really?"

"No." Heather shook her head. "But it's taken us five minutes to go fifty feet, so I figured we should get moving. Just walk normal."

"You realize if I walk normal, you run the risk of me crashing into something or ripping your sweater," I warned her. "I have the ability to collide with objects from several feet away."

She nodded. "I knew the risks when I became your friend," she teased.

When we opened Locker 411, Heather and I both cheered.

"No new clippings!" she said. "Maybe now we'll start getting requests again."

I was also happy to see that the sign-up sheet for the lunchtime's fashion show tryouts was completely full.

Heather texted Brooke while I took down the flyer for the tryouts and went looking for Katie. I found her in the student lounge talking to several girls I recognized from the sign-up sheet.

"But the most important thing to remember is— Oh my God, who died?" Katie's gaze fell on me, and she gasped. The other girls exchanged confused looks as Katie jumped to her feet and ran to me. "Was it your grandma? Which one? Bingo Grandma or Cooks-with-Lard Grandma?"

I gripped her shoulders. "Stop! No one died. What would make you think that?"

Katie gestured to my outfit. "You look ready for a funeral."

"I'm trying to find inspiration," I told her.

She nodded. "Inspiration to never wear that again?"

I stepped closer. "Look, I'm trying to get a feel for what the Lazenby's people like by wearing their clothes."

"Ah. And finding ways to improve them," she said. "Say no more." Katie took my hand and pulled me toward the group of girls. "Vanessa might have something to add to our conversation. Vanny, can you give some ideas on what you're looking for in a runway model?" With a wink, she added, "The girls are a little nervous about all the competition."

"Oh! So you already saw the sign-up sheet?" I asked, holding it out.

Katie nodded. "I checked first thing this morning." She held up a finger. "And you'll be happy to know there weren't any new advice clippings from your friend."

"Well, that's good." I turned to the girls, who were waiting expectantly for an answer. "Okay, let's see. A good runway model should have confidence, good posture, and the ability to walk without falling down." I finished with a smile.

A couple of the girls laughed.

One of the girls raised her hand. "When will you be posting results?"

Katie looked to me, and I said, "Well, we need to take measurements as soon as possible, so you'll know by the end of the day. We'll post the results here in the lounge."

The girls whispered among themselves.

"I'm getting so nervous!" someone said.

"And because we're designing these pieces to fit the models specifically, you'll get to keep them after the show!" said Katie.

Not that they'll want to, I mentally added. But I smiled alongside Katie at all the excitement her comment earned.

When the bell rang for homeroom, Katie joined me on the journey to the sixth-grade hall.

"So how long are you going to dress like that?" she asked.

"Shhh." I put my finger to my lips. "These are Heather's clothes."

Katie smiled. "Aww. Heather always dresses so cute."

I frowned at her, and she waved a dismissive hand.

"Cute doesn't work on you," she said.

I narrowed my eyes. "I know there's a compliment in there somewhere."

Katie put a hand on my shoulder. "You're better than cute. You're sassy and gorgeous."

I smiled. "Good save. And to answer your question, I'll wear this outfit for as long as it takes for me to appreciate"—I took a deep breath—"how wonderful snap buttons are."

Katie gasped and looked me over. "Where?"

In answer, I snapped a button open on the sleeve.

"Oh, what is Heather thinking?" Katie asked, shaking her head.

I said good-bye to Katie outside homeroom and took my seat in front of Brooke's.

"So is the advice box filled to the brim now?" I asked. "Are we going to have to start sending people to 'Dear Abby'?"

Brooke smiled. "No new requests yet, but I checked Locker 411 right before homeroom, and there weren't any new advice clippings, so I think things are looking up!"

Ten minutes later both our phones vibrated. I shifted in my seat so the homeroom teacher couldn't see Brooke, and she checked her messages.

"Shoot!" she said.

"Shh!" the homeroom teacher said, not looking up from a pile of papers she was grading.

Brooke leaned closer to me and whispered, "The Phantom Dirt Digger strikes again!" She turned her phone so I could see the group text that had come through from Tim. Sure enough, there was another clipping from the advice column.

Except this one wasn't in Locker 411.

The Phantom Dirt Digger had struck in the student lounge. And had already gotten some responses.

"Double shoot!" I said.

"SHH!" the homeroom teacher said again, this time looking right at me and Brooke. Luckily,

Brooke was quick enough and tucked the phone up her sleeve as she smiled at the homeroom teacher.

"Sorry. Tough math problem!" she said.

I pretended to work on our imaginary equation while instead writing, *Tell Tim to pull it down before Mary Patrick sees!*

Brooke nodded and started texting but paused halfway through and grimaced. She took my pencil and wrote, *Mary Patrick sees.*

I gave her a confused look, and she turned her phone toward me again with a message from Mary Patrick. It was sent to everyone on the advice team, so my phone was no doubt vibrating in my bag.

First Locker 411, and now the student lounge isn't safe? You'd better deal with the Advice Column Killer.

I pointed at the phone and whispered, "Ooh! I like that nickname." I froze when I realized

Brooke was staring with eyebrow raised. I put a finger to my lips. "I mean . . . shh!"

As soon as homeroom was over, Brooke pulled me aside so we could wait for Heather and Tim.

"Did you see?" Heather asked when she saw us. We both nodded. "What do we do?"

"Spend our days roaming the halls of school, waiting for the Advice Column Killer to strike again." Brooke turned to me. "Yes, it's a better name than mine, okay?"

"We can't waste our time following this kid around," said Heather. "We have classes and choir and runway shows!" She pointed to me.

"And soccer," added Brooke. "At least when the clippings were in Locker 411, we only had one location to watch, but now that this kid's gone rogue, those clippings could be anywhere!"

At that moment Tim showed up, and Brooke

grabbed him by the backpack straps, shaking him back and forth. "Tim! What are we going to do?"

He widened his eyes and freed himself from her grasp while I grabbed her hands.

"For starters we're not going to put Tim in the hospital," I said. "At least not until he's done planning my fashion show."

"Thanks. I think," he said.

"Second, we're not going to panic."

"But nobody's coming to us for advice anymore!" said Brooke. "And Mary Patrick sent me a message saying I'd better come up with a backup plan for the advice team!"

"People will come back to us," I assured her. "This can't last forever. And in the meantime, we still have some older requests we can answer. The important thing is to keep this between us and Mary Patrick, now that she knows. Agreed?"

"Agreed," chorused four voices. I wasn't one of them.

My friends and I turned to see Katie standing behind us, waving.

"What's going on, guys?"

"The Advice Column Killer struck again," I said.

She wrinkled her forehead. "Huh?"

"There was another one of our advice clippings in the student lounge this morning," explained Brooke.

Katie still looked confused. "But I thought they were always in Locker 411. Why the change?"

"If we knew that, we'd be answering advice requests, not fighting our way out of death grips," said Tim. He looked at Brooke. "How are your cats still alive?"

I nudged Katie. "You were in the student lounge this morning. Did you see anyone put something on the bulletin board?"

She frowned. "I wasn't really paying attention,

sorry. But you could ask the other girls if they saw something."

Brooke nodded. "We'll need a list of their names." She seemed to have gotten control of herself and gone into Bossy Brooke mode. "Chances are this kid won't put the clippings just anywhere; it'll be high traffic areas where the clippings will get the most notice. That means the student lounge, the cafeteria, Locker 411, and the restrooms."

"Don't forget the gym," supplied Tim.

"What about the teachers' lounge?" I suggested.

Brooke shook her head. "The teachers would immediately take them down. Plus, it's too risky. We need to be watching those other locations like hawks." She turned to Tim. "Did you already rip down the clipping from the student lounge?"

He reached into his pocket and pulled it out. "Of course!"

Instead of taking it from him, Brooke then turned to me and Katie. "You're holding tryouts in the student lounge at lunch, right?"

We both nodded.

"So, V, I'm putting you in charge of keeping that location cleared," said Brooke. "Check it between classes and watch for any suspicious behavior during your auditions. I'll cover the gym. Tim, you keep an eye on the cafeteria, and Heather, you watch Locker 411."

"What about me?" asked Katie. "I want to help!"

"You can watch the bathrooms," said Brooke.

Katie blushed. "All of them?"

"I'll cover the guys' bathrooms," Tim assured her. She smiled gratefully.

Brooke clapped her hands. "We've already wasted too much time here. Go check your locations and get to class."

I split off from the group and checked the

student lounge. Nothing. I was about to leave when I heard music booming from the far side of the room. I turned and saw Berkeley Dennis turning some knobs on a massive soundboard, complete with speakers that were almost as big as me.

"Whoa!" I hurried over. "Is that for the fashion show auditions?"

Berkeley grinned and nodded while he pushed a few sliders on the board. Suddenly, I could feel the bass in my bones, along with a new wave of excitement. Who cared if he was in sixth grade? My fashion show had a DJ! And he was good!

I nodded along with the beat of the music, imagining lights flashing as my models strutted down the runway wearing . . . pink overalls and lavender turtlenecks.

In my head, there was the sound of a record skipping.

I signaled for him to turn off the music, and

he did so, spreading his arms wide.

"What do you think?"

"It's great!" I said, clapping. "It's just that the fashions are more like this." I pointed to my clothes. "So do you have any calmer music? Like a lullaby?"

He smirked. "Seriously? I figured you'd be designing something funkier. Like what you normally wear."

"I was going to," I agreed, "but the Lazenby's buyer will be looking for something else."

Berkeley scratched his head. "I'll see what I can come up with."

"Thanks," I told him. "And sorry. That really was great music."

"No worries," he said. "DJs cater to the crowd, you know?"

The warning bell for first period sounded, and I pointed to the door. "I should go."

"Right behind you," he said.

I paused. "You're just going to leave your equipment here?"

"Principal Winslow gave me the keys to lock up," he said, pointing toward the door.

I led the way into the hall. "Well, at least I won't have to keep watching the room."

"Huh?" he said, turning the lock behind us.

"Nothing," I said. "See you back here at lunch?"

Berkeley saluted me. "And I'll work on getting those tracks changed for the auditions."

I gave him a thumbs-up but couldn't help feeling a little guilty as he walked away. Before, I was just sacrificing my style for this show. Now I was sacrificing someone else's, too.

That Lazenby's buyer had better bring a credit card to our show.

CHAPTER 5

Walk the Walk

The music from Berkeley's speakers might have been loud, but the chatter of twenty girls hoping for a modeling gig was way louder. Katie and I had taped parallel lines on the carpet about four feet apart to mimic a runway that ran half the length of the student lounge. At the end of the parallel lines, we'd positioned two chairs for us to sit in and do the judging.

Tim tried to sneak in a third chair while he was helping Berkeley with last-minute setup, but I reminded him, with a push toward the door, that he needed to be watching the cafeteria and restrooms for the Advice Column Killer.

"There's a killer in this room right now," he grumbled. "A fun killer. Know what her name is?"

"Don't be silly. Mary Patrick's not in here," I said with a big smile. "Bye!"

When I turned, Berkeley was right beside me.

"Hey, I got busy with school stuff, so I didn't have time to mess with the tracks. The girls are going to have to walk to my original music, but I can change it by the time the show comes around."

"Sure," I told him.

He grinned. "You didn't try to correct me when I mentioned having it ready for the show. Does that mean I got the job?"

I smiled back. "Maybe. Probably. Just get the music going!"

Berkeley chuckled and trotted away. I turned to Katie and gave her a nod. She stood on one of the chairs and waved her hands above her head.

"Attention, you divalicious things! It's time for the runway auditions. All we need you to do is start at the beginning of the runway where Berkeley is"—she pointed to the soundboard and speakers—"and walk down to this end at a casual pace. Turn left, turn right, and walk back to Berkeley. Got it?"

There was a chorus of "Yes!"

But not everyone got it.

One girl walked so fast, I wondered if she imagined herself on fire. Another girl fell down while turning at the end of the runway. She was barefoot.

"Are you okay?" I asked, helping her up.

She examined her nails to make sure they weren't broken and then nodded at me. "It looks like it."

And then there was a girl who turned, left, left again, and left a third time.

"Why is she doing that? Is one of her legs

shorter than the other?" Katie whispered to me.

"Maybe she never learned her right from her left," I whispered back.

After the last girl finally walked the runway, Katie and I applauded, and Berkeley lowered the music.

"Okay, he is seriously good," she said, still clapping. "I want him to just follow me around and mix a soundtrack for my life."

I nodded in agreement. "I think a couple songs will need adjusting, but he's definitely better than a laptop and a playlist."

Katie stood on her chair again. "Thank you, ladies, for coming out. Vanessa and I will review your auditions and let you know later today. For those who get chosen, we're going to ask to meet you tomorrow morning before school to get your measurements."

More loud chatter as twenty girls made their way out of the student lounge. I caught Berkeley's eye and gave him a thumbs-up.

"Make sure you have the new tracks ready by next Thursday's dress rehearsal!" I said.

In response, he cranked the music up and danced in place.

"I think he likes our decision!" Katie shouted to me.

I giggled and pointed to the audition sheets.

"We should really make our choices!" I shouted back.

I motioned for Berkeley to turn the music down, and Katie and I reviewed the models.

Speed Walker, Trippy Longstocking, and Leftie were easy eliminations, along with a few others, but then Katie and I stopped seeing eye to eye.

I was looking for girls like Heather, and Katie was looking for potential ax murderers.

"This one was fierce!" She held up a photo.

"Her eyes were screaming 'I'll eat you alive!'"

"Do we really want fierce?" I said. "Maybe friendly is better. Like this girl." I showed Katie a different photo, and she shook her head.

"That one was too timid. We need girls who own the runway. Girls who own the outfits we put them in."

"But they also need to look like they belong in those outfits," I said. "Your girl looks like she belongs in a straitjacket."

Katie sighed but put the photo in the no pile. "What about this one? Linda? Did you see her sashay at the end of the runway? So divalicious!"

"Too divalicious," I said. "We're trying to say 'Buy our clothes,' not 'You can't afford this.'"

This time Katie didn't put the photo in the reject pile. Instead, she studied me. "What's going on with you? These girls are exactly what we're looking for. And I know for a fact that you've said Linda would make a great runway model."

"For a different line of clothes, maybe," I said. "But Lazenby's doesn't want girls with attitude. I say we go with someone safer like this girl." I picked out another photo.

Katie made a surprised face. "She waved when she reached the end of the runway."

"She was just happy to see us!"

Katie ran her hands through her hair. "Listen, how about we do this? You pick seven girls to model your fashions, and I pick seven to model mine."

"That'll work," I said. "And we'll see which ones get the buyer's attention."

Katie smirked. "If we wanted to do that, we could just put Leftie back in."

By the end of lunch, I'd chosen my models and passed the list to Katie.

"We actually have two in common!" she said.

"We'll have those girls go twice. Once at the very beginning and again at the very end, so they'll have time to change."

"Glad we could finally agree on something," I said. Reaching into my purse, I took out a handful of change and started feeding it into the snack machine.

"Oh, right. We didn't even have lunch!" she said. "Don't you think we should try to grab something healthier from the cafeteria, though?"

"This isn't for us; I need it for Journalism," I said. A pack of Reese's peanut butter cups fell to the bottom of the machine, followed by two more. "It's feeding time at the zoo, and I'm about to face an angry grizzly bear."

Katie wrinkled her forehead. "I really don't get newsroom references."

"My editor's mad because we still haven't caught the Advice Column Killer," I amended.

"Oh." Katie glanced toward the bulletin

board. "Well, it doesn't look like anyone came in while we were here."

"Which means there could be an advice clipping somewhere else with a lot of innocent people on it."

Katie put the audition results into her backpack. "In that case I should check the girls' restrooms. See you after school? We can pin some patterns together."

"Aw, I can't," I said. "I've got to babysit Terrell."

That wasn't exactly true. Terrell was going to be at a friend's for the afternoon, but I needed to get back to Dee's Fabric World to find some milder colors and patterns. Something told me that if Katie didn't approve of my choice of models, she probably wouldn't approve of my new choice of fabrics, either.

"Well, good luck in Journalism, then!" she said. "And if your editor tries to attack, play dead." At the confused look from me, she smiled. "It works with bears!"

The grizzly was all teeth when I walked into the newsroom, but it wasn't because she was going in for the kill. Mary Patrick was standing near Gil's desk actually looking pleased.

"What's going on?" I asked, lowering my bag but keeping my eyes on her. "Why are you so happy?"

Gil glanced up at me and smiled. "Mary Patrick came up with a way to stop the Advice Column Killer once and for all. I've got to admit, she's pretty smart."

"Thank you!" Brooke appeared, dropping into her seat. "I love it when my brilliance is noticed."

"Not you. Me!" said Mary Patrick, poking herself in the chest. "I took care of things when you Floptastic Four couldn't."

"Oh, you don't think we're handling it?" said Brooke, jutting out her chin. "Me and my team are watching all the major gathering places in school and keeping them clippings-free!" She turned to me. "V, have there been any new postings in the student lounge?"

I shook my head.

"Heather!" Brooke called as our friend came through the door. "Any bread crumbs on your trail?"

Heather wrinkled her forehead at Brooke's choice of words. "I didn't find any new clippings in Locker 411 if that's what you mean."

Brooke nodded and glanced around the room. "Well, I think we all know it could be a hundred years before Tim shows up, but if he'd seen any clippings in the cafeteria or boys' room, he would've let me know by now." She smirked at Mary Patrick. "So what do you think of that?"

"Funny," said Mary Patrick. "I was just going

to ask what you thought of this." She produced a small piece of newspaper. "I found it in the library."

Yet another advice column clipping from our favorite fan.

Brooke smacked herself on the forehead. "The *library*! Why didn't Tim think of that?"

"What? Why does all this rage keep happening when I show up?" he asked from the doorway.

"We didn't think to watch the library," Heather filled him in. "And that's where the Advice Column Killer struck."

He cocked his head. "And that's my fault why?"

"You weren't here to defend yourself," said Brooke with a shrug. She rubbed her forehead and sighed. "Okay, not that I'm admitting defeat, but what did you come up with, Mary Patrick?"

Mary Patrick gestured to Gil, who held up a sketch he'd been working on.

"Dun, dun, DUN," he said.

Mary Patrick gave him a look. "I thought we agreed no reveal music."

"Sorry."

Gil had drawn what appeared to be a Wanted poster, but instead of the culprit's face, there was a dark silhouette with the word *BULLY* in the center.

"A Wanted poster?" asked Brooke.

"So far you've only had a few people watching out for the Advice Column Killer, but now the whole school will be!" Mary Patrick crossed her arms in triumph.

Heather pointed at the bottom of the sketch. "We're offering a reward?"

Tim inched closer to the drawing. "How much?"

Mary Patrick's smug smile reappeared. "We won't say. But the mystery of it will keep people interested. And we'll require proof of the culprit being caught in the act."

I nodded. "This is really clever, Mary Patrick. It might even scare the Advice Column Killer into giving up. Especially if he or she knows the entire school is on the hunt."

"That was my thinking, too," agreed Mary Patrick.

All of us turned to look at Brooke, who rolled her eyes. "It's not a terrible idea. But what are we supposed to do until this comes out in the paper? Just let the Advice Column Killer keep ruining people's lives?"

"Oh, we're not printing this in the newspaper," said Mary Patrick. "We're posting this all over school. It ends today." She slapped a palm on Gil's desk.

Now Brooke smiled. "You sound almost ruthless. I like it."

"I've already gotten permission from Mrs. H and the principal," Mary Patrick continued, "so at the end of class, I want you to post these all over campus. Seriously. Every classroom door, every common area, and every pillar. Even on kids who are standing still for too long. I should be able to see one of these everywhere I look."

My friends and I agreed, and Mary Patrick turned to Gil, who got out of his seat and headed for the copier while Mary Patrick headed to the front of the class.

"Man, I'm glad she's on our side," said Tim.

"Yeah, remember when she wanted to get rid of the advice column?" asked Heather. "Now she's fighting to save it."

"Because the advice column is awesome," I pointed out.

"Exactly." Brooke high-fived me. "All right. When she gives us the posters, I'll take the north end of the building. Heather, you can take the east, V can take the south, and Tim can—"

"Take a nap?" he suggested.

The rest of us laughed.

"I thought that's what you're already doing when you're late to everything," I said.

"Only some of the time," he said. "But yeah, I'll take the west wing. It'll be perfect practice for when I work in the White House." He grinned and elbowed Heather. "Get it?"

She nodded solemnly. "I think you'd make a great tour guide there."

Brooke and I snickered.

Since the advice requests weren't flowing in like normal, I did the best with what I had and chose to work on a letter from A Little Different.

Dear Lincoln's Letters,

I love my friends, but we are so different when it comes to clothes and makeup. I like to keep things simple, and they're always dolled up.

They keep telling me I'll never get a boyfriend if I don't try harder, but I'm more worried we won't stay friends. How can I fit in again?

Sincerely,

A Little Different

It was Makeover 101, and I knew exactly what to tell her.

Dear A Little Different,

Congratulations on your first step to a new you! Start by accentuating one facial feature with more makeup and try wearing a new wardrobe piece around the house first, until you're comfortable with it. Think about what you'd like to achieve with this new look, and with that goal in mind, you'll have the boys lining up at your locker.

Confidentially yours,

Vanessa Jackson

“Done with this week’s advice!” I announced, slapping it on Brooke’s desk. As she looked it over, her forehead started to wrinkle.

“Are you sure this is what you want to say?” she asked.

I gave her a funny look. “Yeah, why?”

Brooke read it again. “It’s just . . . I would’ve told this girl something completely different. Sounds like she’s trying way too hard.”

“And that’s why you don’t give fashion and beauty advice,” I said, getting out of my seat and patting her shoulder. “Looking good takes effort, Lazy McSweatpants.”

Brooke sighed. “I should not have shared that nickname with you guys.”

Toward the end of class, my friends and I took copies of the Wanted poster and split up to tackle the hallways. I headed for the south end of the building, and Gil managed to convince Mrs. H to let him come with me. We chatted with each other all the way there.

"Hey, how's the fashion show coming along?" he asked.

"Good! We've got our models picked out, and Berkeley Dennis is going to DJ the event."

"Sweet! So all you have left to do is finish the designs?"

I shook my head and laughed sadly. "No, all I have left to do is *start* the designs."

Gil stopped. "Wait . . . what? I thought you were done with half of them and sewing the rest."

"I need to scrap it all and start over," I told him. "Lazenby's doesn't carry anything like I create. The buyer's going to take one look at my fashions and . . ." I blew a raspberry and made a thumbs-down gesture.

"Are you sure?" he asked. "Maybe she'll really like them. I don't think you should hide your style."

"Oh, I'll still show her my lookbook," I said,

"but if I want to keep her interest, I have to give her what she wants first."

Gil didn't seem convinced. "Do you have enough time to start over?"

I nodded. "It won't be fun, but if I work hard every night and all this weekend, and I don't go too complicated with the designs, I can get it done."

He scratched his head. "Sounds like you're giving up a lot."

"The business world is all about sacrifice," I informed him.

He smiled. "And you know that from your many years of experience?"

"From my mom, actually." I stuck my tongue out at him. "She also told me that boys with long hair are trouble." I flicked his shaggy bangs.

"Well, thank goodness you didn't listen to her," he said, putting his arm around me. "Before you go into fashion hibernation mode, do you want to do something after school?"

I wrinkled my nose. "I can't. I have to go buy yucky fabric."

"I can come with you."

"Really?" I beamed up at him. "That would make it suck so much less!"

Gil laughed. "Of course. And if you need any help with anything else, I can do that, too."

I grinned evilly. "Even trying on some of the finished blouses?"

He leaned closer. "If nobody else ever finds out."

I threw my arms around him. "You . . . are the best boyfriend!"

Now if he only knew how to sew, I'd be all set.

CHAPTER 6

Fashion Cents

"Have you ever been to Dee's Fabric World?" I asked Gil when Mom dropped us off in front of the store.

He shook his head. "I prefer to spend most of my time at Gee's Fabric World."

"There's a Gee's Fabric World?" I turned to him, and he smiled. "Okay, smarty-pants." I poked him in the side. "I just wanted you to know that Dee's is pretty overwhelming the first time you see it."

Gil shrugged. "Eh. It's fabric. I've worn it. I'm familiar with the concept."

I smirked as he opened the door for us. "Don't say I didn't warn you."

Gil didn't respond. Instead, he stared at the shelves and shelves of fabric rolls, all arranged by color, pattern, and type.

"Whoa. Is this where all the colors of the rainbow hang out when they're not working?" He took a few steps toward a shelf and ran his fingers over the fabric. "How do you know which ones to choose? There're so many!"

"Well, those are all for quilting." I gestured to the ones he was admiring. "So I don't use those. We want apparel fabric." I led the way to the far corner, with Gil trailing behind me, touching everything he passed, from spindles of thread to boxes of buttons. I grinned to myself. It was like having Terrell with me.

"Is that my favorite young designer I see?" asked Dee. She was a stocky woman with graying hair and an awesome fashion sense. Today, she had on a red-and-white damask blouse with silky white pants.

"Hi, Dee!" I hugged her, and she peered around me at Gil.

"Who's this handsome fella?" She placed a finger to her lips. "Unless he's not with you, in which case I'd love to introduce him to my granddaughter."

I giggled and blushed. "No, he's with me. This is Gil."

He extended his hand, and she shook it.

"Welcome to Dee's Fabric World," she told him. "Are you here to browse or support?"

"Support," Gil told her.

"I'm getting some extra fabric for the fashion show," I chimed in.

"Ooh!" Dee's eyes lit up, and she rubbed her hands together. "I've got just the thing for you."

She bustled away and returned with a swatch of black fabric speckled with stars and whispers of blue.

"As soon as I saw this, I thought of you," she said.

"It's beautiful!" I said, taking it from her. Already I could see it as a cute dress or flared skirt. "How much?"

"Twenty dollars a yard."

"Oh." My face fell, and I held the sample out to her. For a skirt alone, I'd need two yards, and that was almost all the money I'd borrowed from Mom. "Thanks, but it's a little outside my budget right now."

Dee winked at me. "Why don't you hold on to that sample, sugar? You can always buy the real thing later. For now, we have tons of other options. If you're tight on cash, you can check out the discount area." She pointed to the back corner, and I swore the lighting there seemed darker than everywhere else. "Just help yourself and come see me when you're ready." She smiled and wandered off to greet another customer.

I gazed at the swatch of fabric she'd handed me, but I must have been more transfixed than I thought because Gil nudged my arm.

"Are you sure you don't want to use this for the show? I can loan you some money."

I smiled at him. "Thanks, but even then, it would mean all my designs had the same look. Plus, this pattern is too exciting. I need something that makes me yawn simply looking at it."

I led the way to the discount area, cringing when the cheap fabrics brushed against me as I walked among them. The good news was that everything was under five dollars a yard. The bad news was that it was mainly polyester and spandex.

"What about this?" asked Gil, pointing out a white fabric spattered with pink pompoms.

"A little young," I said. "But you're on the right track."

I scanned some pale yellows and found one with a yellow-and-gray argyle pattern.

"Not my style at all." I wrinkled my nose. "Which means it's perfect."

"Oh, I can top that," said Gil, holding out a stretch of cloth. It was orange with white anchors. "Ahoy, matey!"

"I think that design fell off this fabric," I said with a snicker, showing him one with sailboats.

We both laughed and kept pulling out different, horrible bolts of cloth to show each other.

"Whale, I'll be," said Gil, showing me pink and blue whales.

"This is nuts!" I held up a yellow piece dotted with brown acorns.

"Hue know what?"

"Vanessa?"

Gil and I both turned to see Katie with a

shopping bag, and a frown on her face.

"Oh, hey, Katie!" I shoved the pattern I was holding back on the shelf. "What are you doing here?"

"I'm picking up some more thread for one of my blouses," she said, her frown deepening. "I thought you said you had to babysit Terrell."

"I did! But it turns out I had my days mixed up, so I thought I'd come here and get a little more fabric. We were just goofing off." I turned to Gil. "But now it's time to get serious."

He nodded curtly. "Of course."

Katie broke into a smile. "Fun! Let me help!"

"Oh!" I said. "Um. I think I found the one I want actually." I glanced at Gil for help.

"In your back pocket," he said.

"Right!" I took out the piece of celestial print. "Here it is!"

Katie squealed. "Vanny, this is gorgeous! What are you going to do with it?"

"The same thing I do with all the fabric I buy," I said, talking loudly and looking right at Gil. "Order two yards of it and tell Dee to put it in a paper bag!"

"Is something in your ear?" Katie asked me. "Why are you shouting?"

"What do you mean?" I forced a laugh. "This is how loud I always talk when I am excited about a fabric that is as good as owning five different kinds of fabric!"

I smiled up at Gil, and he smiled back. Katie continued to look at me strangely.

"If you had to buy five different fabrics that were definitely not you, which would they be, Vanessa?" asked Gil in an overly robotic voice.

"Oh, probably the yellow-and-gray argyle, the anchors, the paisley print, the acorns, and the polka dots," I said.

Katie's expression relaxed, and she smiled. "I know what's going on here." She pointed to me and Gil. "You cuties are saying adorable things to each other in some sort of weird couple's code, aren't you?"

I sighed and looked at Gil. "She figured it out, my corduroy sequin."

Gil threw his hands into the air. "Zipper button needle!"

It was all I could do not to crack up.

"Don't worry, your secret code is safe with me," Katie said with an assuring nod. "Because I don't understand it."

I allowed myself a grin. "You're the best!" I told her. "Now let's go look at buttons! They're like the freckles on the face of a shirt!"

I tried to make it sound superexciting, and Katie instantly caught on.

"Yeah! They're going to make your clothes seem out of this world!" She pointed to the piece of star-sprinkled fabric.

"Ha! Good one!" I said.

Katie grabbed my hand and pulled me toward the buttons, and I glanced back at Gil, mouthing, *Thank you.*

You're welcome, he mouthed back, reaching for the argyle fabric.

"So now that you don't have to babysit, let's have a pattern-pinning party!" said Katie. She batted her eyelashes. "Pretty please?"

I grinned at her. "I can't. I promised Gil I'd spend time with him since you and I are about to be so busy getting ready for the fashion show."

Not to mention I didn't have any new designs to turn into patterns, so I was nowhere close to the pinning stage.

Katie pouted and then brightened up just as quickly. "Oh! BTW, the Lazenby's buyer wants to meet next Tuesday."

"What?!" I spun to face her and wound up taking out a display of ribbons with my purse.

Katie's eyes widened and she held up her

hands. "Whoa, what's with demolition mode? All she wants to do is talk."

"Geez." I heaved a sigh of relief and dropped down to pick up the ribbon spools. "Don't scare me like that."

"Sorry," said Katie, bending to help me. "Thank God this wasn't a display of scissors."

"So what does the buyer want to talk about?" I asked.

"Duh, what else? Our fashion show," said Katie. "She wants to make sure we're for real before she commits to coming, so I told her we'd have some pieces ready to show her."

"By next Tuesday?" I fumbled, putting some of the ribbon back on a table.

"Yeah." Katie gave me a strange look. "Why? You said you already have three pieces ready."

Pieces the buyer couldn't see.

But I took a deep breath and nodded.

I had to design, pattern, pin, cut, and sew a

couple of brand-new looks in less than a week. Forget not having time for Gil; I wasn't even going to have time for school!

"Mom, would it be okay if I took the rest of the week off from school?" I asked when she picked me and Gil up that afternoon.

Mom laughed. "Oh sure. While we're at it, I'll throw in a two hundred percent increase on your allowance."

I stared at her until her eyebrows went up.

"Wait, you're serious? Vanessa, what could you possibly need the week off for? You have nights and weekends free, and you got back from winter break not too long ago."

I leaned back in the passenger's seat. "I know, but I'm so swamped with the fashion show and the Advice Column Killer."

Mom swerved the car a little as she glanced

at me. Thankfully, all three of us were wearing our seat belts.

"Advice Column *what*?"

"It's not what it sounds like," Gil spoke up from the back. "The killer is after the column, not the people who write it."

Mom didn't look calmed by this answer.

"Mom. There's no real killer," I said. "It's a figure of speech."

She parked the car along a curb and twisted in her seat to face me. "Vanessa Fay Jackson."

"I swear, it's not a real killer!" I grabbed Mom's hand. "It's just the name Mary Patrick came up with for this kid who's trying to expose people who write in to the advice column for help."

Mom's forehead refused to smoothe out. "Where does the *killer* come in?"

"Nobody's sending in letters to the advice column anymore," I explained. "So the advice column is slowly being killed."

Mom collapsed back into her seat and closed her eyes. "You kids need to seriously come up with a better name than Advice Column Killer or it'll become the Heart Attack Maker."

"Brooke came up with the Phantom Dirt Digger, but everyone liked the other option better," I said.

"Does everyone include parents?" asked Mom, pulling back onto the road. "Also, if nobody's writing in to the advice column, doesn't that give you more free time?"

"Not when I'm spending it trying to track this kid down."

"Well, we did make a little progress today," Gil reminded me. "We started putting up Wanted posters."

Mom shook her head. "I didn't realize we were back in the Wild West. I hope this isn't a dead-or-alive situation."

"Well, Mary Patrick was fine with either," said Gil. "But she had a feeling the principal wouldn't agree."

Mom chuckled. "That sounds like Mary Patrick. Well, I'm sorry you feel buried, Vanessa, but this is part of life. You need to learn to balance your responsibilities, and I know you are fully capable of managing school, the paper, and this fashion show."

"But Katie really complicated things today," I complained. "Now I have to work even harder and faster."

I must have caught Mom on an unsympathetic day. She simply shrugged and said, "You committed to this, V. You need to see it through."

Gil gave me an apologetic smile and hug as Mom stopped the car in front of his house.

"Give me a call if you need any help," he told me.

After we dropped him off, Mom and I traveled in silence for a bit before I spoke up again.

"Can I at least have dinner in my room so I can get some work done?"

Mom regarded me for a moment and smirked. "And I suppose you want to get out of doing the dishes, too."

"If you're offering," I said with my sweetest, most pleading smile.

"I'd better get at least one design named after me," she said. She held up a finger. "And I am not talking about 'mom jeans.'"

I giggled. "It's a deal."

Later, Terrell barely cared that I was carrying a tray of food to my room, because Mom gave him permission to eat in front of the TV. I, meanwhile, wolfed down my dinner and turned my attention to the new fabrics laid out on the floor in front of me.

"What am I going to do with you?" I asked them. Off-the-shoulder numbers were clearly out of the picture. So were crop tops and anything strapless that I didn't plan to cover up with something else. That would take even more time, which I didn't have. While I tried to decide, I changed into my own clothes so I could at least feel comfortable doing something I was going to despise.

I held up the shirt Heather had loaned me and studied it. What I needed to design was something like the shirt.

Or maybe something *exactly* like the shirt.

Could I do that? Take an existing Lazenby's shirt and duplicate it? I didn't have a lot of options with my limited amount of time. Plus, I still planned to show the buyer my lookbook so she'd see what I was capable of. And I'd be putting in all the labor and materials myself.

I turned the shirt inside out and placed it on the floor so I could see where the stitches met. If I traced around the edges, I'd have my pattern right there! Granted, it wouldn't be a new design, but it would be a Lazenby's approved design, and wasn't that really all that mattered at this point?

Now that I had a plan, I was excited to get to work!

I placed the inside-out shirt on a length of the yellow-and-gray argyle fabric and held it taut with my knees while I used a sewing pencil to make the pattern.

Done in less than five minutes.

When I had the lines fairly even, I cut out the length of fabric.

Done in less than two minutes.

I repeated the process until I had two separate pieces for the front part of the shirt. I used pins to piece the whole shirt together and see what it would look like once I'd run it through the sewing machine. It was simple, but it looked almost exactly like Heather's shirt.

And the best part? It had only taken me about thirty minutes to go from the design stage to the showing stage. All I needed now was to get the measurements of my models.

"I might get these shirts done by next week after all!" I cheered to myself.

But I couldn't show off seven variations of the exact same shirt. Even I knew that was ridiculous. I needed a few more designs to mix it up.

I picked up the phone and called Heather.

"Hey, V! What's going on?" she asked.

"Oh, not much." I laid back on my floor. "Have the advice requests started pouring in yet?"

Heather snorted. "No. I don't think that'll happen until we finally figure out who the Advice Column Killer is. How's Project Lazenby's going?"

"Project Lazenby's. I like that!" I said. "And I was wondering if I could borrow a few more of your shirts from there."

"My shirts? Of course," said Heather. "Are you still having trouble getting a feel for the fashion?"

"Actually, I think I've gone as Lazenby's as I can get," I said. "I hope they think so, too."

"That's great!" said Heather. "I can't wait to see how your style meets theirs."

I felt just the slightest twinge of discomfort but fought it back. I wanted to show off my style, too, but there would be plenty of time to make that happen once the Lazenby's buyer fell in love with KV Fashions.

"But I'm only half of KV Fashions," I mumbled.

"What?" asked Heather.

"Nothing. Uh . . . I've got to go. See you at school tomorrow?"

"Sure. I'll bring the clothes," she said. "Bye!"

As soon as I hung up with Heather, I called Katie.

"Hem basting!" she said when she picked up.

"What?" I asked.

"I'm trying to figure out the secret code you

and Gil use," she said. "I took a wild guess that *hem basting* means *hello*. Does it?"

I smiled. "Sure. If you want it to. Listen, I'm calling because we need to meet before school."

"To get the models' measurements. I know."

I shook my head. "Even before then. Just you and I need to talk. And compare progress notes and lookbooks."

"Good idea!" she said. "I've been dying to see what you're working on. Maybe we can meet fifteen minutes earlier?"

"Perfect! See you then!" I told her, and hung up.

I'd been so focused on making sure I impressed the buyer that I hadn't even thought about what Katie was bringing to the runway. And since I was the Lazenby's expert, it was going to be up to me to get her fashions in check.

CHAPTER

7

Model Behavior

But before I could find Katie and chat the next morning, Brooke found me.

"Is it possible to feel like a winner and a loser at the same time?" she asked.

I thought for a moment. "Yes. I felt that way this morning when I found a quarter in the hallway but discovered it had been glued to the floor."

Brooke laughed.

"Why do you ask?"

"Guess how many people have come forward either claiming to be the Advice Column Killer or to have proof of the Advice Column Killer?"

"You know what? I'm feeling good today," I said with a cheery smile. "I'll say ten."

"That's pretty close, actually," she said. "It was eight."

"Great!" I started to wave a triumphant fist, but Brooke stopped me.

"Guess how many of those leads were actually correct?"

I made a face. "Is this where the feeling like a loser comes in?"

Brooke made a zero with her fingers. "One kid claimed to be the Advice Column Killer, but he's been out sick all week. Another kid brought in a friend and claimed his friend was the Advice Column Killer. It turned out they were going to split whatever the reward happened to be. And on and on."

I shook my head. "This is crazy."

"No, it's a catastrophe." She sighed and threw

her hands into the air. "If nobody wants advice, what's the point of having an advice column?"

"People want advice. They're just afraid to ask right now," I pointed out. "We could still help them and not post about it in the paper."

"Well, what fun is that?" asked Brooke.

I rolled my eyes. "Glad to see you're in this for the right reasons."

I headed toward the student lounge, and Brooke followed me. "You know I care about helping other people," she said, "but you've gotta admit that working for the paper won't be as fun if we don't get to see the results."

"Our results will be the smiles of those we've helped," I told her.

Brooke made a face. "You're starting to sound like Heather."

"And what's wrong with that?" asked Heather from where she was sitting with Tim.

"What are you guys doing here so early?" I asked.

"I had choir," said Heather.

"I'm trying to drum up VIP business," said Tim. "But apparently, people in choir do *not* want to part with their money."

Heather elbowed him. "That's because I warned them about what you did with all my change." She looked at Brooke. "So what's wrong with sounding like me, exactly?"

"Nothing." Brooke flopped down beside them and laid her head on Heather's shoulder. "Except I can only take so much feel-good, fairy-tale princess mush."

"Aww." Heather smiled. "You think I'm a fairy-tale princess?"

"You did want to kiss a pretty big frog named Stefan," said Tim. Then he pointed to me. "On a completely different subject, Berkeley told me you asked him to tone down his playlist."

I nodded. "I loved his sample, but the Lazenby's buyer won't. We need music that matches the clothes."

Tim frowned. "I don't know. He played me some of his new stuff, and the clothes that would match, I'm pretty sure you'd buy at a garage sale."

I sighed and rubbed my forehead. "I'll talk to him."

"While we're at it, what did you think of the swag bags Katie and I put together?" Tim produced his planning notebook.

"Oh, the leg warmers are a great idea!" I said.

"Aw, you're doing leg warmers?" Heather asked, pressing a hand to her chest. "Cute!"

"They're going to be printed with a logo Katie and I created." I took Tim's notebook and pen and drew the logo for my friends. "See the *K* and the *V*?"

"Clever!" Brooke said.

"Love!" Heather said.

"What did you think of the actual gift bags?" Tim asked.

"Way to be in the moment," Brooke told him.

I smiled, remembering the tiny purple bags. "They were kind of small. Can we go a little bigger?"

He scrawled a note. "Done."

I thought of the color scheme at Lazenby's. "And can we switch to a different color? Like baby blue?"

Tim's lip curled. "Seriously?"

"What?" I asked.

"It's probably not my place to say it, but KV Fashions doesn't seem like a baby blue empire."

"Baby blue empire. What an awesome name for a show about billionaire babies," mused Brooke. "Wearing little bibs with ties printed on them."

"Aw!" Heather said again.

Tim took back his pen and notebook. "Can we focus? V, I don't think baby blue is a good idea. Purple is much more your style."

"How about we compromise and go lavender?" I suggested.

He started writing. "Fine. Dark lavender."

I stopped him. "Okay, that's just purple. I mean lavender. A *light* purple used on Easter eggs and senior citizen formal wear."

Brooke wrinkled her nose. "Way to sell it, V."

Tim grumbled but crossed out the word *dark*. "At least people will recognize where they are when they see the *K* and *V* cookies."

I leaned closer. "The what? We have our own cookies?"

Brooke tapped me on the shoulder. "I actually helped with that." She smiled in self-satisfaction. "My mom's college roommate owns a bakery, and she offered to give us a few dozen iced cookies shaped like *K*s and *V*s."

"Really?" I couldn't help grinning almost as wide as Brooke. "That's so cool!" I ducked my head a little. "Do you think you could possibly talk her into some *L* cookies, too? You know, to impress the Lazenby's buyer."

"Oh geez," said Tim.

Brooke nodded. "Sure. I can ask."

Out of the corner of my eye, I saw Katie stroll in, and got to my feet.

"I'll see you guys in a bit. I've got to take care of some other fashion show stuff."

"Berkeley's over there if you're looking for him." Tim pointed to a group gathered around a Foosball table.

"Yeah, but I really need to talk to Katie first," I said, pointing toward a magazine rack.

Brooke tugged on my arm. "And *we* need to talk about the advice column. What are we going to do?"

I shrugged. "Until we can figure out who the

Advice Column Killer is, make an announcement in the next issue of the paper that we won't be printing questions, but people can still ask and we'll respond privately."

"I think that's a good idea," said Heather. "That way we can still help! And isn't that the whole point?"

Brooke stared at her. "Is your fairy-tale castle made of cotton candy or chocolate?"

Heather popped her with a throw pillow, and I hurried away before an all-out pillow fight could ensue. Already, Brooke was standing and pulling up her seat cushion.

"Katie!" I called. It was almost like déjà vu. She was surrounded by girls, but these were ones I recognized as the girls who'd tried out for the fashion show and hadn't made it.

Whoops. I guess we should've expected a little fallout.

The girl who seemed to be holding most of

Katie's attention was Trippy Longstockings.

When Katie saw me, her expression seemed almost relieved, and the maniacal way she waved at me confirmed it.

"Vanny! Over here! I've been waiting for you!" *To rescue me*, the panicked look in her eyes added.

"Hey! What's going on?" I asked the group, as if destroying someone's modeling dreams was something I did every day.

"I was just telling Katie," said Trippy, whose real name was Grace. "Everyone's seen the clippings that are going up all over school."

Luckily, I was prepared for this. "Don't worry, the advice column is still going to help people. We just won't be printing the questions and answers where anyone can make fun of them."

"Actually, I was talking about the students being suggested on the clippings," said Grace. "For that question from Beauty Thief, the lipstick shoplifter, I saw quite a few names of girls you have in your fashion show. Is that really the kind of message you want to send? Shoplifting is glamorous?"

Okay, I hadn't been prepared for *that*.

"We don't know if any of them actually did it, though," I said.

"Maybe all of them did it," said one of the other girls.

I shrugged. "Maybe so, but I'm not going to believe any of that until there's actual proof."

"Beauty Thief said she stole a tube of Power Purple," said Grace. "Who's the only girl at this school who wears purple lipstick?" She tapped a snowflake-decorated fingernail against her chin.

"Linda Lee!" someone else piped up.

"Linda Lee," agreed Grace. "One of your runway models."

"Could be a coincidence," I said, but it didn't seem likely. I knew the shade of lipstick Beauty

Thief had mentioned, and it *was* the exact color Linda wore.

"I told the girls I'd talk to Linda," said Katie, "but then they said—"

"What about Erin Moore?" interrupted one of the girls.

Katie gestured to her. "That."

I shook my head. "What *about* Erin?"

"Her name is at the top of the list for the true identity of No Flair, Don't Care."

I remembered that piece. It had actually been a question I'd answered on the website from a girl who didn't see the point of fashion. After I'd pushed my eyeballs back into their sockets, I'd given her a few ideas on how to ease into a love of clothes.

"If she hated fashion, why would she want to be in the fashion show?" I countered.

"Maybe to ruin it," said Grace. "Maybe to make fun of the clothes and models when she's on the runway." Grace shrugged. "Look, I'm not trying to hurt anyone. I just think your models should be passionate about fashion."

"And not be thieves," said one of the other girls.

Katie and I exchanged a look.

"Well, thanks for the concern," I said. "But I'm not going to kick these girls out of the fashion show without proof."

"Me neither," said Katie.

Grace clucked her tongue. "Okay, but don't say we didn't warn you."

I smiled at her and hooked my arm through Katie's. "Can we talk business somewhere private?"

"Absolutely," said Katie, practically pulling my arm out of its socket as she scurried away without even a backward glance at the group of girls. "Holy cow, that was awkward times a thousand! What did you want to talk about?"

"I've made some design changes since I visited the Lazenby's store, and I think maybe you should, too."

Katie raised an eyebrow. "I am having a seriously weird morning. Why would I want to change my fashions?"

"So they're more in line with what Lazenby's wants." I produced my cell phone and showed her one of the shirts I'd been working on. "Like this."

"Ugh. That's hideous!" Katie made a face like she'd sniffed sour milk. "How much did you pay for it?"

I lowered my phone and frowned. "I made it."

Katie's eyes widened, and she pressed her lips together. "You know, it's growing on me the longer I look at it." She reached for my phone, but I held it at arm's length.

"Look, I know it's horrible. You don't have to lie to me," I said, and Katie blushed. "But this is the kind of stuff Lazenby's carries. You really think they'd be happy with one of mine?" I scrolled through the photos and found one of my own finished pieces, an off-the-shoulder black number trimmed with blue velvet.

Katie gasped. "That is gorgeous! Yes!"

"No!" I replied. "They'd never carry something like this in their stores. Trust me, I checked. And that's why I'm making new designs just for them. And you should, too."

Katie fidgeted with the zipper of her sweater. "But I want the buyer to see my current stuff."

"And she can," I assured Katie. "After we've won her over with what she wants to see, you can show her the other amazing things you have to offer."

Katie gave me a dubious look. "There're less than two weeks until the fashion show. I won't have time to come up with seven new designs and sew them before then!"

"Sure you will. I'll help." Suddenly, I had a flash of brilliance. "And so will Brooke and Heather!"

We had our weekly movie night coming up. I was sure the girls wouldn't mind doing something a little different for a change.

"I don't know, Vanny." Katie frowned. "I think we've got a pretty good chance with what we've already designed."

I put a hand on her shoulder. "Katie, trust me. I write an advice column about this stuff. I scouted the store. I talked to someone who works there. We need to nail the Lazenby's look or we don't stand a chance with them."

She looked less uncertain, so I decided to sweeten the deal.

"We can have a sewing sleepover," I sing-songed.

It sounded like something old people would do, but Katie's frown shifted into a smile. "A sleepover? Fun!"

I nodded. "We can even have Heather and Brooke try on the tops we make and hold a pre–fashion show fashion show!"

Katie bounced up and down. "Count me in! I'll bring my portable sewing machine! And popcorn!"

"Heather will love you for that," I said with a grin. "So work on your designs right now, and on Saturday, we'll have the sleepover and get all the sewing done. Then next week we can do fittings and a practice run."

"Don't forget the meeting with the Lazenby's rep," said Katie. Then she smiled. "That sounds so professional to say."

I smiled too. "Then it's settled. New fashions that cater to Lazenby's style and a sewing sleepover!"

"Yay!" said Katie as the bell rang to start homeroom. "I'll catch you later!"

"Watch out for wannabe models," I warned her, only half joking.

When I got to homeroom, I told Brooke about my run-in with Grace and the other girls and then about the sewing sleepover. Brooke frowned through both stories.

"Okay, first, I seriously doubt Grace is thinking of anyone but herself, and second, I don't know how to sew. But if you're okay with me stapling the fabric together, I'm all over that."

"I can teach you," I said. "And you're probably right about Grace. But she might be right about Linda and Erin, too."

"So what if she is?" asked Brooke with a shrug. "The Lazenby's buyer isn't interested in the models; she's interested in the clothes. You could probably dress up some mannequins on wheels and roll them across the stage."

I wrinkled my forehead. "You don't understand the point of a fashion show. The models are there to display the clothes at their best. They add depth, reality, and an extra layer of beauty."

Brooke raised an eyebrow. "And you want *me* to make the clothes?"

I laughed. "Like I said, I can teach you. And worst-case scenario, you can thread needles the whole time."

She smirked. "Maybe you can give sewing advice to the whole school since we won't have any new material to put in the paper."

"You joke," I said, "but that's not a bad idea. We could at least do it until the mess with the Advice Column Killer dies away."

"I think we should be more worried about how Mary Patrick's going to act when she realizes we don't have any new requests."

But when we walked into the Journalism

room that afternoon, Mary Patrick didn't so much as glance at us.

"I can't believe she hasn't thrown a desk at one of us," I said. "I just checked the advice box, and it's empty."

"Because I have the requests right here!" declared Heather with a cheerful smile. She gestured to a pile of papers.

"Wow, for real?" I picked up one of the requests. "'Dear Lincoln's Letters, I have trouble smiling in photos. As soon as the camera flashes, I'm frowning. What can I do? Mona Lisa.'" I brightened. "That's not a bad one! And there's nothing superembarrassing about it, so the Advice Column Killer won't bother to post it."

"This one either," said Brooke, flicking a piece of paper. "'Dear Lincoln's Letters, How can I convince my parents to let me get my ears pierced? Girl with a Pearl Earring.'"

“And I’m working on a request from Starry Night, who wants to know if taking a girl to the planetarium is a lame date,” said Heather. She returned to her writing, humming to herself.

“Hey, maybe our problems with the Advice Column Killer are over!” Brooke told me.

I didn’t answer. Something seemed off about these requests.

The name Starry Night reminded me of a Van Gogh painting called *The Starry Night* that I’d talked about once with Gil and Tim. The *Mona Lisa* was a painting, too, by Leonardo da Vinci, that Tim had mentioned the other day.

I pulled out my phone and did a search for “Girl with a Pearl Earring.”

A painting by Johannes Vermeer.

“Hey, team! What’s going on?” Tim strolled into the classroom and threw his bag onto the desk.

I faced him with arms crossed. “You tell us,

Van Vinci Vermeer. We're on to you." I nodded at Heather and Brooke, who stared up at me, blank-faced.

"Huh?" said Brooke.

"Yeah, what are you talking about?" Tim gave a nervous laugh but avoided meeting my stare.

"I'm talking about the batch of advice requests that mysteriously appeared this afternoon. They all seemed to be signed by kids who chose famous works of art as their secret identities." I pointed to the pile that Heather and Brooke were now sifting through.

"'The Scream,'" read Heather.

"'The Last Supper,'" read Brooke.

"'The Great Wave.'"

"'Washington Crossing the Delaware.'" Brooke pounded her fist on the desk and glowered at Tim. "Seriously?"

He shrugged. "I figured you guys would be too excited to see advice requests to notice. And like I've said before, it wouldn't hurt this school to be exposed to more culture." He pointed to me. "But I'm impressed you knew they were pieces of art *and* that you knew it was me."

I smirked. "There aren't many kids at our school who are big into art. And only one who knows the advice column is hurting for questions."

Tim squinted at me and then nodded. "Nicely done. You could give the Young Sherlocks a run for their money."

"Hey!" said Brooke. She balled up the request she'd been working on and threw it at him.

He caught it and opened it. "Well, don't throw this away. It's still a good question!"

"Not from someone who really needs help, though," said Brooke. "And you know our rule about writing our own requests."

He nodded. "I do. That's why I didn't write

them. Plus, I didn't want Mary Patrick to see they were all written in the same handwriting. So I had guys on my basketball team do it last night."

"I was wondering why none of the signatures looked familiar!" Heather was scanning several slips of paper in front of her.

I glanced over at Brooke, expecting her to leap over her desk and throttle Tim, but she just studied him.

"You had a bunch of people write requests for you?"

"Yeah," he said with a subtle step backward.

"All from the basketball team?" Brooke asked in a soft voice, still watching him.

Tim took another step back and whispered to me, "I haven't seen this version of Brooke. Is she about to reach into my chest and rip out my heart?"

I shook my head. "She's thinking."

"Oh," he whispered again, relaxing. "That's new."

Brooke's expression turned to one of annoyance.

"That look isn't," he said.

Brooke stuck her tongue out at him and looked at me. "V, do you have the list of people that signed up for the fashion show auditions?"

I blinked in surprise. "Uh . . . yeah." I reached into my bookbag and pulled out my fashion show project binder. "Here you go." I handed her the sheet of paper from the front pocket.

"What do you need that for?" Heather asked while Brooke read over the names.

Brooke held up a finger and looked at me again. "Who were the girls you were talking to this morning? The ones who didn't make it into the show?"

I rattled off their names, and Brooke put a

check beside each one on the audition sheet. Then she pulled out a couple of the clippings the Advice Column Killer had posted.

Heather glanced from one of the clippings to the audition sign-up sheet. "You don't think . . ."

"Yep," said Brooke.

Tim and I exchanged a confused glance.

"What is it?" I asked.

Brooke turned the sign-up sheet and one of the clippings to face me. "Tim had a team do his dirty work for him. What if the Advice Column Killer had a team do her accusing for her?" She pointed to the sign-up sheet. "Notice any familiar handwriting between this and the list of people accused of being No Flair?"

I looked at both documents and frowned.

One of the girls who'd auditioned, Georgia Riddle, dotted the *I*s in her name with big circles. On the list of the accused, the *I* in Erin Moore's name was dotted with a big circle. A different model signed her name in all caps. On the list of the accused, I saw the name of one of the selected models in all caps.

"Some of the girls who tried out were trying to make the others look bad," I said.

Brooke nodded. "And the Advice Column Killer asking the questions is . . ."

All it took was a glance at the sign-up sheet. "Grace."

Tim smiled and put his hands on his hips. "And just think, you wouldn't have figured it out without my fake advice requests. You're welcome!"

I got to my feet. "I'm telling Mary Patrick."

But when I brought her over to show her what we'd discovered, she didn't look as confident as the rest of us. "You might be right, but you can't make an accusation like that without more proof. Did you catch her in the act?"

"No, but—"

"And why did she switch from using Locker 411 to the bulletin board?" pressed Mary Patrick.

I pounded my fist on the table, and everyone jumped. "I got it! She was following the list of models wherever it went. We started with the names in Locker 411, and then we switched to posting them on the bulletin board."

"Excellent deduction," Brooke said, high-fiving me.

"What about the one in the library?" countered Mary Patrick.

"That's where Katie and I typed up the list of models who made the cut. Grace must have seen us in there."

Mary Patrick didn't look as impressed. "You still need more proof."

"Fine," I said. "Then let's focus on catching Grace in the act."

CHAPTER

8

To Catch an Advice Column Killer

One of the amazing things about middle school is how fast news travels. Even made-up news. By Friday morning it was all over school that the girls selected to model for KV Fashions were also meeting a talent scout who could launch their modeling careers!

I of course told Katie and the models it wasn't true, but nobody else knew except the advice column team and Mary Patrick.

I printed up the fake flyer and posted it on the board in the student lounge early that morning. Why? Because if Grace wanted to destroy the lucky girls, I was certain she'd do it in the same location their success was being announced. I just had to catch her in the act.

Luckily, I happened to be dating a boy who was a photographer, which meant he knew all kinds of camera tricks, including how to turn a smartphone into a motion-detecting camera using just an app.

"Whenever someone approaches the bulletin board, it'll record fifteen seconds of footage," said Gil. "Hopefully, whatever Grace is going to do, she'll do within that time frame." He held out his hand, and I gave him my phone.

"I have a feeling she'll get in and out as quick as possible," I said. "She wouldn't want anyone to see her."

Gil placed my phone on a bookshelf and hid everything but the lens. "Any time someone approaches the bulletin board, you'll get an email, along with the recorded footage."

"Have I ever told you how amazing you are?" I asked.

Gil smiled a dimply smile. "Yeah, but I never get tired of hearing it."

He and I settled on a couch near the bulletin board, where we could see who came in and noticed the bulletin board.

"Are you excited to meet with the Lazenby's buyer next week?" he asked.

"Excited and nervous," I said. "I hope she likes the new designs. Especially with all the extra work we're putting in to make sure they're Lazenby's material. We're even having a sewing sleepover this weekend so we can have samples done in time."

Gil scratched his head. "I think she'd like your original designs better, but if she *does* like the new ones, is that really what you want to be known for?"

I shifted to face him. "What do you mean?"

He took one of my hands in his. "You've got lots of talent, V, but your first show isn't, well, *showing* that. You're bringing out some fake Vanessa that you think people want to see. Not the real one they came to see in the first place."

I stiffened and pulled away from him. I knew there was a compliment hidden in there somewhere, but the mention of me being a fake kind of stung.

"Don't worry about me. I've got this under control," I told him.

He nodded readily. "Of course you do. But maybe when you meet the buyer next week, after you show her the acorn blouse and anchor tank top, you could show her some of the stuff you were working on *before* you knew she was coming?" His smile was so hopeful and cute, I couldn't resist returning it.

"Well, I was gonna do that, anyway," I said. "But I suppose it wouldn't hurt to meet her actually *wearing* some of my designs."

"My girlfriend, the world-famous designer." Gil beamed and settled back as Brooke and Tim approached.

"My boyfriend," I replied with a giggle. "The world-famous photographer."

"My breakfast," said Tim, "coming back up any minute." He pretended to gag as he flopped onto a chair beside the couch.

"Always a delight to disgust you," I told him.

"Has the hook been baited?" Brooke asked in a low voice, sitting on my other side.

"If you're asking if I posted the flyer, then yes," I said. "And we've got a camera set up to record whoever stops at the bulletin board."

Brooke gave a low chuckle and rubbed her hands together. "Good, good. Time to disgrace Grace."

I looked at Gil and pointed to Brooke. "This is why you never want to get on her bad side."

Tim leaned toward us, planning notebook in hand. "Now that we've gotten that taken care of, Vanessa, I came up with some more stuff for the VIP swag bags. I'm ordering custom M&M's with the letters *KV* on them, but I need to know what colors you want. I'm thinking green and platinum." He winked. "Money colors."

"What about gold?" suggested Brooke.

"What about no?" I said. "Tim, are we getting these candies for free?"

"Don't worry about it." He waved a dismissive hand. "I've got a guy."

"A guy?" I repeated.

"My uncle," he admitted with a sheepish grin. "He wanted to help because he thinks it's great that you and Katie are pursuing your dreams."

"Aw, that's so sweet of him! Give him a hug for me."

Tim nodded. "He's started wearing deodorant, so I'm okay with that. Now, what colors?"

"Green and platinum are fine," I said. "Or . . . wait . . ." I reached out a hand to halt his writing. "Lazenby's is more into pastels. Maybe pink and lavender?"

Everyone around me wrinkled their noses.

"Don't make those faces," I said. "What is wrong with catering to the customer?"

"Haven't you already done that enough?" asked Gil. "You already changed your designs. That's plenty."

I shot him a warning look.

"You changed your designs?" asked Brooke. "To what?"

"You'll see tomorrow when you're sewing them," I said.

"You can sew?" Tim asked her.

"No, but apparently, it's easy to learn," said Brooke. "After this weekend I'll be able to perform open-heart surgery."

The rest of us laughed.

"Moving on," said Tim, checking his notebook again. "How are the custom leg warmers coming?"

"Shoot!" I clapped a hand onto my forehead. "I forgot about those."

"Ehhh," Tim made a buzzer sound. "The correct answer is 'I'm working on them, and they'll be ready by next Friday.'"

"They will be ready by next Friday," I agreed. "I mean, how many VIPs can there be?"

"Fifteen."

My eyes widened. "Fifteen? That's a lot!"

"That's awesome!" said Brooke. "I figured my parents would pretty much be half the VIP section."

"Aw, you had them get VIP tickets? That's so sweet!" I squeezed her.

"Of course! You're my best friend!" she said.

"Heather got VIP tickets for her family, too."

I grinned. "Can you imagine Heather's grandma in leg warmers?"

We all laughed.

Gil elbowed me. "Not to brag, but I bought a VIP ticket, too."

I leaned over and hugged him. Then Gil, Brooke, and I looked at Tim expectantly.

"I did not purchase a VIP ticket," he said, typing something into his phone, "because I am your event manager. I won't have time to sit." He put his phone down. "By the way, I talked to Berkeley for you, and we found a music selection we think you'll like. Not as intense as EDM but not as lame as Top 40."

"EDM?" I repeated.

"You know. Electronic dance music," Tim said, as if that was common knowledge.

I gave him a skeptical look. "Send me a sample, anyway."

“Already on the way.” He wiggled his phone at me.

“Speaking of on the way, Grace is on her way to the bulletin board,” said Brooke in a low voice. “And it looks like she’s taking the bait.”

I stretched as casually as possible and glanced around. Grace and a couple of the girls I’d seen yesterday were reading the flyer I’d pinned up. At any moment they were going to look my way. I turned to face Brooke.

“Grace is looking over here now, isn’t she?”

“Yep,” said Brooke. “And she is not pretty when she frowns.”

“I have a feeling it won’t be very long before the Advice Column Killer strikes again,” said Gil.

He was right.

At the end of homeroom Brooke and I went back to the student lounge to look at the bulletin board. And right next to my flyer was an advice column clipping from our friendly neighborhood

Advice Column Killer. This one was about a girl who was afraid of the dark and still slept with a nightlight.

Who is In the Dark? was scrawled across the top in Grace's handwriting, and underneath that, also in Grace's handwriting:

Vanessa Jackson

"Wow, she isn't holding back, is she?" asked Brooke.

"That's okay," I said, pulling down the clipping. "Because her five seconds of fame are over." I reached up into the bookshelf and retrieved my cell phone.

"Did we get her?" Brooke watched over my shoulder as I pulled up my email.

There were several emails from the monitoring app, which made sense with the student lounge being a busy area. I ignored the ones from before the start of homeroom, since my friends and I had been watching the bulletin board at that point. After those, only two more alerts showed up. The first one was Mary Patrick, who must've gotten out of homeroom to make sure I'd done my part.

The next video was of Grace tacking up the advice clipping next to my fake flyer.

"Busted," said Brooke, giving me a high five.

I pocketed the advice clipping and clutched my phone to my chest like it was a pair of Prada pumps. Then Brooke and I headed for the principal's office.

"I can't believe I'm here again," said Brooke. She'd been sent to see Principal Winslow not long ago, after breaking into the science lab and trying to start a fire. For good reasons.

"At least you're not in trouble this time," I pointed out.

The secretary regarded us with a wary eye. "Good morning, ladies. You're about to be late for first period."

As if on cue, the warning bell rang.

"We're here to see the principal," I said. "We know who the Advice Column Killer is."

The secretary sat up straighter. "'Killer'?"

I really needed to remember not to use that word around adults.

"Bad nickname," said Brooke, stepping forward. "I prefer Phantom Dirt Digger."

The secretary didn't look any more relieved.

"The kid who's been posting the advice column clippings and getting kids to rat out other kids," I tried again.

"Ah," she said with a nod, picking up the telephone receiver. She punched a button and said into the mouthpiece, "I've got some students to see you about the Newspaper Bully."

A moment later the principal's door opened, and he stepped halfway out. When he saw us, he grunted. "If it isn't the riot starter and the fire starter."

The riot starter was me. Back when girls had been fighting over my makeup kit in the Van Jackson days.

I held out my phone. "We know who did it, and we have proof."

By Friday afternoon, there was a last-minute write-up for Monday's paper, assuring readers that the Advice Column Killer had been caught and would no longer be a menace. After Principal Winslow saw the video footage, he had a private conference call with Grace and her parents. Grace had to promise she wouldn't post any more clippings or spread vicious rumors. And she and her friends went to every kid in school that they'd accused and apologized, including ones like Ryan Durstwich, who they'd included just to keep things from looking too fishy. No doubt Ryan had dragged out the apology and maybe even tried to get them to do chores for him, like he'd done to Tim.

On Friday night I finished pinning my patterns, and on Saturday evening I was pacing in my driveway, waiting for my friends to come over. Since Katie lived across the street, I spent most of my time staring at her front door until she finally opened it, bag in hand.

"Sewing sleepover!" I chirped, charging at her.

She laughed and held up her hands. "I actually came out to tell you that I'm still getting my stuff together. But I thought I'd keep you busy with some new fabrics!" She held out the bag.

"Ooh. Let me see!" I reached in and pulled out a length of pink gingham. "Oh. Hm."

I knew it was Lazenby's style, but it was just so . . . not mine. Or Katie's.

"Yeah," she said. "I tried to remember those

pictures you had posted up in your room. My dad thought I'd hit my head or something when I chose this fabric."

"It's okay," I assured her. "We can get back to our own designs next weekend. For now, we've got"—I reached into the bag and pulled out some white eyelet—"a buyer we have nothing in common with to impress."

A car horn honked, and we both jumped.

"Where's the party at?" Brooke called from the passenger window of her mom's van.

Katie and I both waved, and Katie jiggled the fabric bag at me. "I'll be over in a few minutes. Just let me grab my sewing machine and sleepover stuff."

"I've never heard anyone put those two items in the same sentence," I said with a grin, taking the bag. "See you in a few!"

I ran back across the street to help Brooke

with her sleeping bag while she pulled a duffel from the backseat.

"Bye, Mom!" Brooke shut the car door.

"Bye, sweetie! Have *sew* much fun!" Her mom called through her open window. "Get it?"

"Yes," Brooke said with a groan as her mom honked again and drove away. To me, Brooke added, "There have been many puns since I told my parents the theme of the sleepover. My dad's favorite? 'You *seam* like you could do it.'"

I giggled. "That's actually cute."

"If you say *sew*," said Brooke.

And we both laughed.

"Come on." I motioned toward my house. "My mom sent Terrell to a friend's for the night, so we have the whole downstairs to ourselves."

"Awesome!" she said, following me up the driveway. "With pizza, I hope?"

"Of course." I put her sleeping bag and Katie's

fabric bag down in the front hall. "Mom! Brooke's here!"

"Hey, Brooke, sweetheart!" Mom called from the kitchen.

"Hi, Mrs. Jackson!" Brooke clapped her hands together. "Okay, when do the sewing lessons begin?"

"Um . . . we can start now," I said. "Let me just get some fabric scraps for you to practice on."

I ran to my room, and when I came back, Mom was hugging Heather's mom while they brought in Heather's stuff.

"I wasn't sure if you needed an extra sewing machine, so I brought my *bubbe*'s old one," said Heather.

Brooke and I glanced past her.

"Is it invisible?" asked Brooke.

"No, it's heavy," said Heather's dad as he hefted it inside. "Where should I put it?"

I removed some magazines and coasters from the coffee table. “Right there should work,” I said.

After he’d gotten it situated, I turned to Heather. “Do you know how to use that thing?”

“I can do basic stitches,” she said while her parents followed Mom into the kitchen for coffee. “But if you want buttons, I’ll have to sew those on by hand.”

There was a knock on the front door before it opened a crack. “Vanny, can I come in?” asked Katie.

“*She* has a sewing machine, too?” Brooke asked when Katie put her bags and machine on the floor. “Great! I’m the only person who doesn’t have one.”

I patted her shoulder. “I think you’re better off sewing by hand, anyway.”

“Yeah,” agreed Heather. Katie nodded too.

“What do you mean?” asked Brooke.

"Well, sewing is a delicate art," I said.

"I can be delicate!" said Brooke. "This morning I drank orange juice with my pinkie out!"

"That's dainty, not delicate," I said. "And I have a feeling that if I put you in front of my sewing machine, you'd destroy the needles or the fabric or both."

"But you can use the scissors!" Heather told her with a big smile, holding out a pair of shears.

Brooke took them from her. "You know, you guys underestimate me. All of you." She waved the scissors at each of us in turn.

"Maybe you should've started with a pincushion," I said to Heather.

Brooke stuck her tongue out at me and put the scissors down. "You don't think I can use a sewing machine? Try me."

Heather and Katie watched for my reaction, and I handed Brooke the piece of practice fabric. "If you can sew a straight line of even stitches without breaking anything, I'll let you use my sewing machine and *I'll* do the sewing by hand."

I placed my sewing machine on the coffee table next to Heather's. "The bobbin and needle are already threaded, and the knobs are set for a medium straight stitch. Go for it."

Brooke gave me a simpering look as she sat on the couch in front of it. "Well, you still have to teach me how to use it."

"Fine," I said. "Start by lifting the foot and putting the fabric under it."

Brooke glanced down at her legs. "Which foot?"

"The foot of the sewing machine," said Katie.

"The sewing machine doesn't have feet," said Brooke, staring at the base of the machine.

I pointed to the metal piece in the middle of the machine that had the needle suspended above it. "This is the foot." I lifted it for her and put the fabric underneath before lowering the foot back down. "Now, when you put one of *your* feet on the pedal, it'll feed the fabric through."

Brooke tentatively pressed on the pedal, and the machine whirred to life, the needle pressing stitches into the fabric and pulling the fabric under the foot.

"Whoa, neat!" she said with shining eyes.

"Put your hands on both sides of the fabric to guide it," I said. "But don't get your fingers too close to the needle."

Brooke did as I instructed, and for a second, I thought she might actually be able to sew a top using the machine.

But then she said, "Can't this thing go any faster?" and started pumping the pedal with her foot. The machine whirred and stopped. Whirred and stopped.

"It's not a race car," I said. "This is as fast as it goes."

"Bummer," she said, pressing the pedal down

and pulling the fabric under the needle so that it started skipping stitches.

"You don't need to do that," I said. "It goes through on its own."

But Brooke kept pulling. With her other hand she fiddled with one of the knobs. "You only have this set on three. I'll bet if you cranked it to—"

The thread snapped, and a second later, the needle started to bend.

Heather winced, and Katie hid her face in her hands.

Brooke lifted her hands and took her foot off the pedal, slowly sliding away from the machine. "You know, I think I'd be really good at cutting fabric," she said, not daring to meet my eye.

"I think that's a good idea," I said.

Brooke cleared her throat. "Does anyone know where I put the scissors?"

It was going to be a long night.

Once Brooke found the scissors and was

given patterns to cut, she actually turned out to be pretty useful. I think because she was trying extra hard to redeem herself after almost murdering my sewing machine. Heather took care of basic stitches for all the garments, and Katie and I put the finishing touches on them. Then we had Brooke and Heather model for us.

"This is so cute! Can I keep it afterward?" asked Heather after she put on a top I'd made.

"You can even model that one in the fashion show if you want," I told her with a smile. It was nice to know at least one person was enjoying my creations.

"This collar's really choking me," said Brooke, pulling on it.

"That's because you've got the shirt on backward," I said.

Brooke glanced down. "No, I don't. Look at the buttons."

"They go on the back," I said.

Brooke gave me a crazy look while she unfastened the shirt. "That doesn't make any sense. How am I supposed to dress myself if the buttons are behind me?"

I shrugged. "Get a maid?"

For now, I buttoned the shirt for her, and she frowned at herself in the mirror as she turned to look at herself from the front and back. "This doesn't look right. It's like my head is on backward."

"That would explain a lot," I said. Katie and Heather giggled.

Brooke didn't. "I've never seen you wear anything like this. Why did you change your designs again?"

"To get the buyer to like us," I told her. "First, we show her what she likes, and then we show her what *we* like." I gestured to myself and Katie.

With Heather's and Brooke's help, we were able to get six pieces ready for the buyer.

“You guys are the greatest.” I gave both my friends a squeeze when we were done. “KV Fashions will forever be in your debt.”

“Hear! Hear!” Katie said, raising her glass of soda.

“Just win that buyer over,” Heather told us. “That’s all we ask!”

Brooke cleared her throat. “That, and for a fashionable line of sweatpants.”

She quickly found herself buried under a pile of pillows.

CHAPTER 9

Buyer Beware

On Monday morning the first thing my friends and I did was check the bulletin board in the student lounge for new advice clippings. Thankfully, Grace seemed to be staying true to her word.

During homeroom Katie and I met with our models so we could fit the garments we'd loosely put together for them. I watched their expressions as they tried on each piece, but nobody seemed to have any issues with the designs.

"What do you think of the tops you're wearing?" I finally ventured to ask.

"Oh, they're great!" said Linda.

"Yeah, I didn't think I'd look good in gingham, but I do!" said someone else.

I beamed. Katie and I were definitely going to blow that buyer away.

On Monday night we did the alterations for the tops we'd made and talked about what we'd be wearing the next day to our big meeting.

"Gil thinks I should wear something that's more my style and not Lazenby's," I said. "So I thought I'd wear the vintage tuxedo jacket that I cropped into a bolero, with the yellow blouse I made."

"Ooh. That sounds adorable!" said Katie. "I'll wear my pencil skirt and the red cap-sleeve with the black lace overlay that *I* made."

"We're gonna look so professional!" I said. "Do you think we should show her our look-books first or the actual samples?"

"Actual samples," said Katie. "Show her we

mean business and we're not just little girls doodling in our notebooks."

"Good point," I said. "What if she asks about pricing?"

Katie grinned. "You think she's going to instantly fall in love with our stuff?"

"Wouldn't you?" I asked.

Katie scooted closer with an excited bounce. "Okay, well, we have to think about how much the material costs and how much time it takes."

I thought for a moment. "So, if the fabric costs about ten dollars a yard, and we need two yards for a shirt, that's twenty dollars right there. How much do we charge for the work?"

"Thirty dollars?" suggested Katie.

I made a face. "So we're going to ask them for fifty dollars a shirt? That seems like a lot of money."

"For one of our fashions? Please. They're lucky we don't charge them double!" she said with a wink. "But worst-case scenario, we could always work with a distributor."

"A distributor?" I repeated.

"You know, someone who'll make our shirts and put them in stores for a cut of our profit," said Katie. "Which might work out better for us, since we won't really make any money if we have to sew these all ourselves. Plus, they'll have storage facilities so we don't have to turn our bedrooms into tiny warehouses, or worry about shipping."

I sat back and chewed on my fingernail. "Wow, there is a lot of stuff to this business I didn't think about."

"My dad can help us with all that after we get our contract," Katie assured me. "For now, I noticed something missing in all our samples." She pointed to the inside collar of a shirt I made. "No shirt tag with our logo on it."

"You're right!" I picked up the shirt. "Do we

have time to order some?"

Katie laughed. "Not by tomorrow afternoon! We'll have to settle for sewing our logo into the shirts."

And that's what we did.

On Tuesday morning I slid the outfit I planned to wear for the buyer into a garment bag (no way I was risking stains or wrinkles), along with the samples I'd made over the weekend.

"Good luck, sweetie!" Mom kissed me on both cheeks as I headed out the door. "And don't sign any paperwork without talking to me first!"

I hugged her extra hard for thinking it might get to that point. It's always nice to have people who believe in you.

Principal Winslow agreed to let us use the student lounge after school for our meeting with the buyer, so that afternoon Katie and I spread our samples on a long table, along with our lookbooks and some business cards Katie had printed. When she and I had first met, I remember thinking how ridiculous it seemed that a twelve-year-old had business cards, but now I was grateful at how professional she was.

Heather, as a Lazenby's clothing lover, had agreed to stand outside the student lounge and bring the buyer in, so Katie and I found the most businesslike chairs in the room and wiggled in our seats, waiting to shake hands with our future.

Right on schedule, the door to the student lounge swung open, and Heather stepped through with a tall brunette woman. For some reason I'd expected her to be wearing Lazenby's spring line, but she was in dark skinny jeans, silver flats, and an emerald-green cold shoulder top. Her hair was done up in a sloppy bun, with a few strands that played around her red, rectangular glasses, and a red leather jacket was draped over one arm.

I so wanted her wardrobe when I grew up. Heck, I wanted it right *now.*

"Ms. Stone, meet Katie Kestler and Vanessa Jackson," said Heather, pointing to us in turn.

The woman offered her hand. "Please, feel free to call me Michelle."

"I love your look," Katie told her, shaking Michelle's hand. "Can I be you for Halloween?"

I cringed, but Michelle laughed and shook my hand next. "You know, I've never been asked that. It's oddly flattering."

Well, the good thing was I couldn't say anything more embarrassing than Katie.

"Hi," I told Michelle with a nervous smile. "Your shirt and jacket look like Christmas."

Or could I?

Michelle gave me a strange smile, and Heather

stepped closer. "These two are really into the holidays, in case you can't tell," she said. "Why don't you guys show Michelle what you've been working on?" She gestured at the contents of the table.

"Yes, I'm the new buyer on the block for the company, so I'm eager to see what you've made for your fashion show," said Michelle, sitting in the chair opposite me and Katie. "I see you're familiar with what Lazenby's already carries." She eyed our designs. "But what do you have to offer that's new?"

Katie and I smiled at each other.

"Actually, these clothes that you think are Lazenby's were the ones we made," I said.

Michelle picked up one of the tops. "These six pieces are what you've got for your fashion show?"

"Oh, not just these," said Katie. "We're still

finishing some more, but you can see them here." She flipped open our lookbook, past our original designs, to the Lazenby's ones.

Under the table, Katie and I held hands and watched.

Michelle glanced at the first design and said, "I believe I've seen enough." My heart hammered in my chest, and I tried to not have my smile too ready. If we were going to talk money, it was best not to seem too eager. Something I'd learned from my mom.

"Ladies," said Michelle, "as much as I admire your handiwork, there's nothing here I haven't seen a hundred times before. I think I'm going to have to pass."

Katie and I unclasped hands and glanced at each other. Then we both leaned over the desk toward Michelle.

"Sorry, what?" I asked.

"You're passing?" added Katie. "Does that

mean the same thing in your world as it does in ours?" She pointed from herself to me. "Because passing is good in school!"

Michelle gave us an apologetic smile. "It means Lazenby's won't be carrying your line. But thank you for the opportunity to meet! Maybe in a few years, we can try again."

I shook my head, still confused. "You're still coming to the fashion show, right?"

"I'm sorry, no. I wouldn't have a reason," said Michelle, getting to her feet.

Katie just stared at her, openmouthed. I fumbled to pick up the lookbook.

"But these styles are exactly what Lazenby's has!" I stabbed one of the pages with my index finger. "We're giving you exactly what you want!"

Michelle pressed her lips together. "I'm afraid you're wrong. Right now our clothes have limited appeal to kids, but we're hoping to improve the existing collection. We've also hired a spokesmodel, Trinity Fawn, for that reason. I was hoping when I met you, that you'd be more in touch with what kids want." She frowned. "But it doesn't seem that way."

Out of the corner of my eye, I saw Katie's head slowly turn so that she was staring at me. Heather was watching me, too, lower lip tucked between her front teeth.

This whole misunderstanding was my fault. The Lazenby's buyer didn't want more of what they had; she wanted something different.

And I was something different. So was Katie. But I'd thrown out our unique styles and made us just like someone else.

Michelle picked up her purse and started for the door.

"Uh, wait!" said Heather, stepping in her path. "They have more designs! Better designs!"

"Yes! Right here!" I flipped to the front of the

lookbook where our original designs were and thrust it at Michelle. She smiled and stepped around Heather. "Excuse me. I have several more appointments to get to." She pointed to her watch.

I hurried around the table. "You said you were hoping we'd be more in touch with what kids want, and we are! We were just trying to give you what we thought *you* wanted."

Michelle put a hand on my shoulder, the weight of it like a thousand disappointments. "You don't change your style to suit someone else, sweetie. You find someone whose style matches yours." She withdrew her hand and lowered it to shake mine. "It was lovely to meet you girls."

"I upcycled this from an old tuxedo jacket!" I pointed to my bolero.

"Very nice," said Michelle. Her friendly smile was starting to grow thin as she placed her hand in mine and squeezed it. "It was a pleasure. Keep working on defining your style."

She reached for Katie's hand next, but Katie crossed her arms and tucked her hands under her armpits, as if that would keep Michelle from leaving.

"We have our own styles!" she insisted.

"We just wanted to be in your store so badly," I added.

Michelle sighed and scratched her head. "I'm not sure I can explain this any better. The clothing you made is lovely, but it's an imitation of someone else." She pointed to the table with its pile of rejects that I felt a sudden urge to burn. "Lazenby's wants to buy original designs from original designers. Now, I really have to go."

She started for the door again, and Heather moved to open it for her but then paused and stepped aside with her hands behind her back. As Michelle left, the door closed with a click, but it might as well have slammed with an echoing thud.

Katie and I were frozen in place, staring at our dream that had just walked away in incredibly fierce flats.

Heather approached our table. "Are you guys okay?" she ventured.

"The Lazenby's buyer just left," whispered Katie. "I can't believe it."

"She doesn't think we're real designers." I dropped down into my chair. "We're frauds!"

"No." Heather came around to my side of the table and knelt beside me. "That is not true," she said firmly. "The two of you are *not* frauds, Vanessa."

I nodded slowly. "You're right. We're not frauds. Just me."

Heather grabbed my hands. "V."

"I'm only twelve, and I'm already giving up what *I* want in order to be what other people want," I said. "Who will I be by the time I'm an adult? A dentist in a clown costume?"

Heather rocked back on her heels. "That is incredibly weird and specific."

"They're two of the things I *least* want to be," I told her. Heather squeezed my hands.

"How do you think *I* feel?" asked Katie. "Yeah, you let someone affect your decisions, but I let someone affect my decisions who was letting someone else affect their decisions. If anyone's more of a fraud, it's me!"

I got up and reached for Katie's hands. "I'm so sorry. This was the dumbest idea I've ever had!"

"It's okay," she told me with a rueful smile. "I've had dumb ideas, too."

Heather put her arms around both our shoulders. "At least you had good intentions."

"And look where good intentions got us today." I held up the lookbook before I chucked it into the trash. "We should've stuck with what we love," I told Katie. "And if someone else didn't like it, so what?"

"Yeah!" she said. "We don't need that stupid Michelle, anyway!"

The door to the student lounge opened, and all three of us spun around.

"Michelle, I'm so glad you came back!" cried Katie.

But it was Brooke who appeared.

"Hey, guys!" she said. "How was the meeting?" She took in our expressions. "Uh-oh. Did the buyer not like the samples?"

"She didn't like *us*," I said. "She thinks we're posers."

Brooke's eyes widened. "What? She said that to a couple of kids?"

"Well, she said our clothes were just imitations and not showing our styles," corrected Katie. "And the sad thing is, she wasn't wrong."

Brooke nodded. "I didn't want to say anything, but yeah. The clothes we were sewing were nothing like the fun ones you normally make."

Even though the situation was dismal, I couldn't help smiling.

"You think our clothes are fun?"

"Of course! They display your personality." Brooke picked up one of the shirts. "But these clothes say, 'When I grow up, I want to run a yarn store.'"

Katie giggled, and Heather said, "Hey! I like that top."

Brooke threw it at her. "Then take it. Better yet, take them all." She tossed the rest to Heather. "Katie and Vanessa don't need them anymore."

Katie held up a finger. "Actually, we kind of do. For the fashion show."

I groaned and buried my face in my hands. "The fashion show. A lineup of clothes I don't even want to promote."

"So don't," said Brooke. "Isn't it *your* show?"

I lifted my head. "Yes. Yes it is!" I clapped a

hand onto Katie's shoulder. "Hey, now we can do whatever we want! We don't have to show off those clothes. Nobody outside this room knew what our final lineup was!"

Katie started to smile, but it fell into a frown. "We don't have anything for our models to wear. The pieces we fit them for are awful Lazenby's designs."

"Hey!" Heather said again with her head poking out of one of the tops.

"We'll come up with something," I said. "This is our first-ever fashion show, and people are going to see what KV Fashions can do." I picked up my phone and dialed Tim. "It's time to get real."

CHAPTER 10

Happy Accident

"Let me guess. You're calling to ask all your friends to change their names to Lazenby," said Tim when he answered the phone.

I rolled my eyes. "No."

"Just me?"

"*No.* But I *am* calling to ask you to make some changes."

Tim sighed. "Vanessa, I swear if you want me to make the doilies on the snack table any doilier . . ."

"Doilies? Gross. Go with foil cardboard cutouts," I said. "And take the *L*s out of the plates of

K and *V* cookies. Also, go with purple for the gift bags. Dark purple. Like a painful bruise."

"V, seriously, your analogies are terrible," said Brooke.

I shushed her with a look. "And if we can afford it, I want neon glow necklaces on every chair," I told Tim.

He was quiet for a moment. "Brooke's with you, right? Can you put her on the phone?"

She looked just as baffled as I felt when I passed my phone over to her. Brooke listened for a moment and said, "No, Vanessa didn't fall and hit her head this time. Not an evil twin, either. I'm pretty sure she'd be the evil twin, anyway," Brooke said with a wicked grin at me.

"Give me that!" I snatched the phone back. "Tim, can you put things back to the way they were or not?"

"Shouldn't be too hard," he said. "But why did you suddenly change your mind? Did the

Lazenby's buyer turn out to be different from what you thought?"

I smirked. "Actually, *I* turned out to be different from what I thought."

I told him what happened, and Tim sighed. I could practically picture him smoothing his hair back in frustration.

"I'm sorry, V. I should've said something. I knew you weren't being you, but I got so caught up with turning this thing into a moneymaker. I'm sorry."

"Don't be," I said. "You were just being yourself and doing what you love, which is what I should've been doing. I just hope it's not too late to get back to that. Does Berkeley still have the first mix he made?"

There was a muffled sound, followed by [illegible]uting a question to someone away from [illegible]econd later the volume returned. [illegible]y says he still has it."

I breathed a sigh of relief. "Tell him I'm sorry for all the extra work he put in to change it, but we'll be going with the original instead."

"No problem. It's good practice!" I heard Berkeley shout when Tim conveyed the message.

"Well, I should really get off the phone," he said. "I've got a lot of calls to make."

"Sorry," I said again, biting my lip.

"Don't worry about it," said Tim with a smile in his voice. "I'm just glad you're back to normal. Well, as normal as you can be."

When I got off the phone with him, I called my mom to come pick us up.

"Hi, honey! How was the meeting with the buyer?"

"I'll tell you about it when you get here," I said.

"Uh-oh. That doesn't have a whole lot of promise to it."

"It's okay," I said. "Things didn't turn out

quite like I wanted, but Katie and I are still going to throw one heck of a fashion show."

This time when I got off the phone, Katie was waiting with her hand raised. "Question. You might have heard me mention this earlier, but how are we going to throw a fashion show with no fashions? We've only got two days until the dress rehearsal, and I don't know about you, but I've only sewn a few of my original designs."

"Maybe we could have another sewing sleepover?" I suggested, glancing at Heather and Brooke.

Both of them looked at each other, and Heather spoke up first.

"I'd love to help, but there's no way my parents are going to let me go to a sleepover on a school night."

"Yeah, and sewing isn't really my thing," said Brooke. "Not until you get a machine with more horsepower. And sharper scissors for the fabric.

Like those ones on the infomercials that can cut a pizza—and anyone who tries to steal the pizza—in half."

"My dad works for a textile company," Katie reminded me. "He might know some people we could hire to do the sewing for us."

I shook my head. "We can't afford to pay anyone. My mom wouldn't let me skip school last week, but maybe she'll let me do it this week."

That didn't go over well when Mom picked me and my friends up.

She interrupted me before I even finished my question.

"The solution to your problem isn't to make more problems for yourself," she said. "And trust me, getting behind in your schoolwork will only make more problems."

"Then what am I supposed to do?" I moaned, and flopped back against the passenger seat of the car as dramatically as possible.

"You learn from your mistake and move on," she said.

"But this is a really big one," I said. "I can't start my fashion career this way."

Mom chuckled. "Honey, that's how everybody gets ahead in this world. You make mistakes and you learn and you evolve." At the pout from me, she squeezed my leg. "The very first time I tried to sell a house, I locked myself, *and* some potential buyers, on the balcony. And the property was on the twentieth floor."

My friends and I giggled.

"I remember that story," I said with a grin. "You threw your right shoe at the neighbor's back door. But nobody came out to help."

She nodded. "So I threw my left shoe at the other neighbor's back door."

Everyone in the car laughed.

"But I learned from that mistake," said Mom.

"And after that, I always made sure to keep an extra key on me."

"And an extra pair of shoes?" I teased.

Mom chuckled again. "The point is that you're going to survive this, honey." She winked at me. "And someday, you can tell people your story and laugh."

After Brooke and Heather were dropped off and Katie was back at her house, I went up to my room and studied the designs I'd been working on. I had the three tops I'd completed before the Lazenby's disaster started. If I hurried and didn't care too much about the stitches, I could maybe have two more done by Friday *and* I could throw in two of the better pieces I'd made for Lazenby's.

Mom agreed to let me eat in my room again, and while I shoved half a sandwich in my mouth, I prepped my sewing machine for top number four. I would never confess it to Brooke, but at that particular moment, I did actually wish I could make the machine go faster.

I tried to multitask, running the fabric under the needle with one hand while I flipped through my original lookbook in search of what would be the quickest pieces to make. I found a design that seemed pretty promising, but since I couldn't get up to find a bookmark, I simply set the acorn shirt on top of the page. The leather cover closed over it, and the shirt fanned out above and below the edges.

With the brown leather accenting it, the shirt didn't look half bad.

And it gave me an idea that was all good.

I stopped working on top number four and disappeared into my closet. On one of the shelves, I kept a box marked "Scraps," and after a bit of digging, I found a piece of the dark-brown leather left over from my Halloween costume. It was thin and flat enough to sew onto something else, and luckily, there was just the right amount of it left for what I had in mind.

Taking some quick measurements, I cut two squares and two strips from the fabric. Then I sewed each square onto a shoulder of the shirt and attached the strips lengthwise down the sides under the armholes. Now the shirt was sweet *and* sassy. More my style.

I took a picture of it and texted it to Katie.

What do you think? I asked.

After a moment, she responded with OMG! Is that the acorn shirt? So cute!

Right? You know what this means? We don't have to make all new clothes! I typed excitedly.

Instead of texting back, Katie called.

"Are you suggesting we upcycle our own creations?" she asked when I answered the phone.

"We've got the skills," I said. "And we can

definitely make a few tweaks here and there in two days, no problem."

Katie gave an excited squeal. "Vanny, you are brilliant! And I've got all kinds of stuff we can use!"

"Me too!" I said.

There was a fumbling sound, followed by Katie breathlessly saying, "I'll be right over!"

I looked at the clock and then laughed. "You're crazy. It's almost ten o'clock. Our parents would kill us."

Katie laughed too. "I guess you have a point. I'm just so excited!"

"We'll meet before school tomorrow," I told her. "Bring a box of your best decorative pieces, and I'll bring mine, and the shirts. We can figure out how to fix each one and save this fashion show!"

Katie cheered, and we said good-bye. I turned to get back to my sewing and saw Mom standing in the doorway with a big smile on her face.

"Learn and evolve," she said. "That's my girl."

It was way too loud in the student lounge to hear ourselves think. And it was partially Tim's fault. He was seated on top of a table, surrounded by a sea of girls, but for once they weren't gazing at him adoringly. They were gazing at the rows of shiny purple bags on either side of him.

"Why won't you tell us what's in them?" one girl asked.

"If you come to the fashion show on Friday afternoon, you'll find out," he said with a wink. "But trust me, there's gold in here." He patted one of the bags.

"There's gold in there?" a girl screeched, and reached across the table.

"Not actual gold," Tim said, holding her at arm's length and rolling his eyes. "I mean the stuff inside is really great."

Katie and I looked at each other and grinned.

"You gotta give him a gold star for trying," she said.

I clutched at her arm and gasped. "An actual gold star?"

She laughed. "I feel like we're kind of giving away the big finale if we work on the clothes here," she said. "Maybe we should go somewhere else."

I nodded. "Good idea. I think the newsroom is pretty empty in the mornings. If you're willing to brave Mary Patrick."

"Oh, she doesn't scare me," said Katie, picking up her box of fashion flair. "I know you think of her like a bear, but to me, she's more like a growling dog that's missing all its teeth. You just want to pet her."

"Yeah, I wouldn't recommend that," I said, leading the way out of the student lounge. Out of habit, I stopped at the advice box and peeked through the slot to see if there was anything inside. I saw a couple pieces of paper. "Woo-hoo! Looks like we might be back in business."

"Yay!" said Katie.

"You'd better be," Mary Patrick's voice carried from inside the newsroom. "Because Brooke has terrible suggestions for what to do with the column if the requests completely stop."

Katie drew her lips over her teeth and growled. I snickered quietly and stepped into the room.

"What were her other suggestions?" I asked Mary Patrick. She held up a piece of notebook paper.

"We could have a recipe column, where kids write in with their favorites." Mary Patrick regarded me with dull eyes. "Do you know how many twelve-year-olds would submit their top secret formula for toast?"

I smiled. "Hey, slap a little butter on there, and it's delicious."

Mary Patrick shook her head. "If I didn't like the recipe column idea, Brooke also suggested a cat corner, where everyone could send in pictures and drawings of their cats. Does she not remember that I'm allergic?"

I raised my eyebrow. "To pictures of cats?"

Mary Patrick sighed. "Anyway, why are you here?"

"We actually wanted a quiet place to talk fashion," Katie spoke up. "And aside from your occasional complaining, this place works great!"

Mary Patrick narrowed her eyes at Katie. "Do you own cats?"

"I own a hamster named Queequeg," said Katie, placing her box on a desk and opening it. "But I'm allergic to cats, too."

Mary Patrick watched her for a moment and then went back to frowning at the note from Brooke.

Katie and I shrugged at each other, and I took the first shirt we needed to fix out of the bag. "The pink gingham tank top!"

"Ugh!" Katie made a face. "It's even pinker than I remember! It looks like something a giant toddler would wear."

"Okay, so we need a way to make the color not stand out as much," I said. "And we need to age it up a bit. What says 'I'm older'?"

"Gray hair," mumbled Mary Patrick.

"Not helpful," I shot back, but Katie's eyes lit up.

"Actually, something like that might work. The color, I mean."

Katie rummaged through her junk box and pulled out a packet of iron-ons. "What about this silver crest for the center of the chest, and silver rhinestones spaced evenly around the armholes and neckline?"

She placed the crest on the shirt and plucked a couple of rhinestones from a Ziploc bag, setting them along one of the armholes. "I'd have to get some more rhinestones, of course, but that'll only be a couple bucks."

"Yes! That looks *so* much better," I said.

"You're welcome," added Mary Patrick.

Katie and I moved on to the next shirt and the next, pulling brilliant ideas from the boxes until we actually made it a race to see who could come up with the better solution first.

While we worked, Tim strolled in, grinning from ear to ear.

"I sold three more VIP passes to the fashion show this morning," he said, fanning himself with the dollar bills. "Peer pressure is a beautiful thing."

"Wow, people really want what's in those bags," said Katie.

"What *is* in them, by the way?" I asked.

Tim leaned back to glance out the door and then spoke in a confidential voice, "Custom M&M's with your initials, provided by my uncle Theo; lip gloss, provided by Brooke's parents; temporary henna tattoos, provided by Katie's parents; glittery nail files, provided by your mom." He pointed to me.

"Tim, you are seriously awesome for putting this all together!" said Katie, giving him a high five.

"I'm not done with my list," he said with a smile but still gave her the high five. "The VIP bags also have compact mirrors with a shoe design on the cover, provided by Heather's parents, and leg warmers provided by you two." He pointed to me and Katie, and my heart stopped.

The leg warmers. I'd completely forgotten

about the leg warmers.

From the way all the color left Katie's face, I could tell she had, too.

Tim eyed us both suspiciously. "Okay, I'm feeling a lot less of the happy from you two than I was a second ago."

Katie turned to me and raised her hands to her cheeks. "We didn't make them!"

"I know!" I said. We both turned to Tim. "We don't have the leg warmers ready now," I said. "And we won't have them ready by Friday, either."

Tim eyes became alarmingly round. "What? They were the central appeal of the VIP bags!"

I wrung my hands. "Well, we have the mirrors and the nail files and—"

"That's all dollar store junk to make people feel like they got a lot of stuff," Tim scoffed. "We need those leg warmers!" He hammered his fist into his palm with every word.

"We're barely going to have time to redo these pieces," said Katie, holding one up.

"Then you need to give me something else," said Tim. "How long does it take you to make a handkerchief?"

It was my turn to scoff. "Nobody carries a handkerchief these days, Grandpa."

"What about mittens?"

"They'd take even longer than leg warmers," said Katie.

"Plus, it's almost spring," said Mary Patrick from the front desk.

Tim dropped into a chair, and all of us sat in contemplative silence. Except for Mary Patrick, who was humming as she liberally applied a red editing pencil to someone's article.

"Hello?" There was a knock on the doorframe, and I glanced over to see Grace skulking in the doorway. Mary Patrick looked even less pleased to see her than I was.

"Why are you saying hello like you're not sure if anyone's here?" she asked Grace. "You can see us, can't you? What do you want?"

Grace stepped forward. "To talk to Vanessa." She smiled tightly at me. "I just wanted to make sure you're not going to mention my name in the article about the Advice Column Killer."

I stared at her. Then I laughed. "Seriously? That's what you're worried about after you hurt other people? Yourself?"

Anger flashed in Grace's eyes, and she put her hands on her hips. "I already apologized, so it's not like people don't already know it's me."

"Then what are you worried about?" asked Tim.

"I just don't want people to be *reminded* that it's me," said Grace.

I snorted with disbelief. "Well, don't worry. We won't ruin your good name like you ruined other people's."

Grace looked from me to Mary Patrick. "Promise?"

"*Yes.* We've got more important things to worry about," I said.

Tim cleared his throat and turned to Grace. "You wouldn't happen to be really good at making leg warmers, would you?"

"You're joking." She actually had the nerve to fix him with a derisive stare. "And risk messing up my nails? Hard pass."

There was a loud clap from the front of the room that made us all jump, followed by the forward charge of Mary Patrick.

"I knew I recognized you!" She pointed at Grace, who blinked and backed up several paces. "We had an article in our paper about you last year. You're really good at nail art. You decorate your nails for every holiday." She grabbed one of Grace's hands and pulled it toward her. Sure enough, the snowflakes were gone, and now her nails sported smiling hearts on them.

"So?" Grace jerked her hand back, and Mary Patrick looked at me and Katie.

"That's your extra item for your VIP swag bags. A gift certificate. Grace is going to offer to do nail art for all the VIPs."

"No I'm not!" Grace protested.

Mary Patrick nodded. "Yes, you are. Because after what you pulled, you owe this newspaper a favor for endangering one of its sections. Especially when we're being nice enough *not* to draw more attention to what a jerk you are."

Grace turned red. "What, so you're blackmailing me now? If I don't help, you'll ruin my life?"

I shook my head. "No. No blackmail. If you don't help us, nothing bad will happen."

"But you *will* do this," said Mary Patrick. "Because it's the right thing to do."

"Plus, you probably have really bad karma right now," added Katie. "You might want to get rid of some of that." She fanned the air.

Grace glared at Tim, who held up his hands. "You're not up for the challenge. I get it. Anything beyond basic cutting and taping of newspaper articles *can* be tough."

"It wouldn't be a challenge," said Grace with a snarl. "I can go to a slumber party and do five sets of nails like that." She snapped her fingers.

"By my count, there are probably fifteen VIPs who will cash in their certificates," said Tim.

Grace's eye twitched, but she nodded. "Fine. But after this, we're even." She stared at me until *I* nodded.

"Agreed."

Grace stormed from the room, and Katie called out, "Your karma is looking cleaner already!"

Mary Patrick faced the doorway, arms

crossed in smug satisfaction. "That takes care of *that*."

I smiled at her, the growling dog missing all its teeth. But instead of petting her, I gave her a hug.

And she didn't try to bite me.

CHAPTER 11

Vanessa on the Runway

Katie and I finished brainstorming fashion changes at lunch while Tim eyed us nervously.

"You look like you're waiting for one of us to have a heart attack," I finally said. "What gives?"

"I just want to make sure there won't be any last, *last*-minute changes," he said. "Because I'm pretty sure the lady at the bakery is going to push me into the oven if I go back to her again."

"We're sticking with what we've got," I said, crossing my heart with my finger. "And we will be ready for dress rehearsal tomorrow."

Katie nodded her agreement. “But I do wish we could’ve put more of our original fashions in the show,” she said with a wistful smile.

“Here’s something that might cheer you up,” said Brooke. “Well, it cheers *me* up, anyway. Advice requests have started coming in again!” She let a handful of paper slips flutter down onto the lunch table, even more than the ones I’d seen that morning.

Heather, Tim, and I pounced.

“Please tell me your friends didn’t write any of these,” I said to Tim.

He shook his head. “If they did, it was because they really had questions this time.”

“I’m so glad we can help all these people again!” chirped Heather.

“I wonder if they missed asking us for advice as much as we missed giving it,” mused Brooke.

“Probably,” said Tim. “We do give some really good advice. If I may say so myself.”

"You may," said Brooke. Heather giggled.

"Let's face it," continued Brooke. "We're hardly ever wrong. Right, V?"

I didn't answer right away. I was thinking about Tim's declaration of our advice-giving skills. He was right; we *were* pretty amazing, but Brooke was also right. While we were hardly ever wrong, we *were* wrong occasionally.

Like with my advice to A Little Different.

I'd given her tips to get in good with her new fashionista friends, but I was also telling her to not be herself. Just like I hadn't been myself with the Lazenby's buyer.

"V? You okay?" asked Heather.

"Yeah," I said with a smile. "Just thinking."

"About changing the fashion show?" asked Tim with an alarmed expression.

"No," I said. "About the advice I gave in our last column. Brooke, you were right. I said the wrong things, and I wish I could change it."

Heather put her head on my shoulder but just as quickly sat back up. "Hey, maybe you could write an article where you take back what you said! What do they call it?"

"A retraction," said Brooke, frowning. "I don't think Mary Patrick would go for that, though. It would look bad for the paper to admit they were wrong about something."

"Would it?" asked Tim. "Or would it look better that we admit we're not perfect? It could be a great think piece."

I leaned in eagerly. "Ooh, I'd really like to do that. I don't want A Little Different to end up like us." I gestured from me to Katie, and she blinked in surprise.

"You mean awesome and with great hair? I think everything turned out a-okay," she said.

"Yeah, but that was after we suffered the humiliation of realizing we should've just stuck with our own styles," I said. "I don't want it to be my fault if someone else goes through that."

"Maybe it already happened," said Brooke with a shrug.

The rest of us booed her.

"You really think that makes me feel better?" I asked.

"I'm just saying, you might be wasting your breath. Just let it go and don't give that advice again."

But I couldn't let it go. Whenever I thought about what I'd told A Little Different, I cringed. Two minutes into the start of Journalism, I raised my hand, interrupting one of Mary Patrick's rants about how sacred her red editing pencil was and demanding its return.

"Do you have my pencil?" she demanded.

"Uh, no. I was just wondering if the *Lincoln Log* ever printed a retraction," I said.

"V, don't," whispered Brooke.

Everyone in class turned to stare at me.

Mrs. H blinked in surprise but said, "We've printed corrections, but I don't think we've ever done a retraction. Why do you ask?"

I rubbed my incredibly sweaty palms across the table. "There's a first time for everything, right?"

People murmured to one another, but all eyes still watched me.

"What is there to retract?" asked Mary Patrick in a voice that sounded almost hostile. I tried to remember Katie's comparison between Mary Patrick and a toothless dog. "Did you lie?"

"Of course not!" spoke up Heather. "Vanessa doesn't lie."

"I didn't lie," I agreed, swallowing hard. "But I didn't give the right advice, either."

Now the entire room was talking, but they weren't bothering to keep their voices down.

"I like how the advice column brags about how great they are, and now they want to print a retraction," said Felix, the front-page team's leader. "Are you wanting to retract *that* claim?"

Several students laughed, but I didn't care.

"No, I'm not retracting that claim, because we *are* great," I said, fixing him with an even stare. "I just want the chance to give the right advice to our readers." Now I looked to Mrs. H and Mary Patrick. "Sure, A Little Different, that girl I wrote to, may be the only one in that situation right now, but next week it could be someone else. And they'll remember what I wrote, and I'd like what they remember to be what's right."

Mrs. H smiled. "I think that's wonderful."

"Me too," said Mary Patrick.

The room got as quiet as if she'd let out a bloodcurdling scream.

"What?" she asked, blushing. "I mean, okay, I wouldn't have called it 'wonderful.' More like pathetically endearing."

"How are you not the most popular girl in school?" Tim asked her.

"My point," said Mary Patrick, "is that I agree we should fix this now. People believe what their news source tells them, and it's up to us to maintain our integrity and make sure we repay their loyalty." She nodded to me. "Come up with something by Friday, and if you need help, let me know."

"Thanks," I said, feeling loads lighter already.

Between that and tailoring my tops into something I could live with, the week was turning out better than it had started. What made me even happier was sharing our new designs with the models at Thursday's dress rehearsal.

"Oh my gosh, are these the same things we tried on Monday?" asked Linda. "They look amazing!"

I smirked. "So they didn't look amazing before?"

She blushed and ran her fingers over a leather shoulder piece. "Well, I mean, they were good before, but now they're even better!"

"They weren't good," I said with a smile. "But thanks for being sweet."

"Vanessa?" Brooke appeared wearing the top she was modeling. This time, facing the right way, with the buttons in the back. "I thought I figured this shirt out, but now the armholes are really tight, and there's all this extra sleeve fabric left over."

I laughed. "Those aren't armholes. They're for your shoulders. Your arms come out through the bottom of the sleeves."

Brooke laughed, too. "Phew! I didn't want to be the one to tell you that this design was terrible."

Luckily, the rest of my models didn't have as much trouble, and soon, they were lined up at the entrance of an imaginary stage, ready to walk the walk.

I signaled to Berkeley, who cued up his music, and then Katie nudged the first model forward. I motioned for her to slow down so the imaginary audience could admire the top, and I admired it myself. We really had turned things around.

It gave me more confidence to write my retraction for the newspaper.

I handed it over to Mary Patrick on Friday morning, and her frown didn't appear once as she read it. Neither did her red editing pencil, which she'd found mysteriously hidden in the trash can.

"This is good," she said. "And very professional." Mary Patrick slid the letter into her notebook. "I hope I'll feel the same about your fashion show."

"You're coming?" I asked, unable to hide my surprise.

"I'm the editor of the school paper, and that's the biggest thing going on this week," she informed me. "Plus, I heard a rumor that VIPs get free nail art."

I giggled. "Well, thanks for your support. We'll do our best to impress."

"I'm impressed right now, actually," said Mary Patrick. "You seem really calm for someone who's making their fashion debut in eight hours."

"It's just for family and friends," I said with an easy smile. "Everyone in the audience already loves me."

But as four thirty drew closer, the nerves started to set in. I kept checking and rechecking everything that had to be done before the fashion show to make sure I wasn't forgetting anything.

I sent Tim a text during history while the teacher set up a DVD for us to watch.

Did you get gift certificates from Grace?

Tim leaned over. "You know I'm sitting right next to you, right?"

"Yes, but I'm nervous!"

He gave me a reassuring smile. “Relax. I’ve got it all under control. You just make sure the chairs are set up around the folding platform.”

I started to nod but then stopped. “The what?”

“The folding platform the models will be walking on,” he said. His jaw dropped. “You *did* set that up with the school custodian, didn’t you?”

“No!” The panic rose into my voice.

“I’m just kidding. I took care of it,” he said with a rakish grin.

I clutched a hand to my chest while he snickered. Then when I was sure my heart was beating normally, I smacked his arm. “Don’t do that! And *did* you get the gift certificates?”

“Of course,” he said. “The VIP bags are all ready to go, and my parents will be coming at four thirty to set up the food.”

"What about the music?" I asked.

Tim clucked his tongue and sighed. "Berkeley traded his sound system for a banjo. Can the girls sashay to 'Yankee Doodle'?"

"Give me your other arm," I said. "I want your injuries to match."

He laughed. "Quit worrying, V. Everything is taken care of. All you have to do is make sure your models are ready to hit the runway and then bask in the glory of the audience's applause."

I liked that image. But it would've been nicer if the audience could see the kind of stuff Katie and I really worked on.

And maybe they could.

I asked the history teacher for the bathroom pass and hid in a stall to call Mom.

"Hi, honey! Is everything okay?"

"Yep," I said. "And if you can do me two favors, things will be even better."

* * *

One foot. *Scrape.* Six inches. *Scrape.* One foot.

I climbed onto the runway platform and looked down at the chairs I'd arranged for the audience. They seemed a little far apart.

I hopped back down and sat in one of the chairs, eyeing the runway. Then I scooted the seat closer to the one beside it and sat in *that* one.

"This is the saddest game of musical chairs I've ever seen," said Brooke from behind me. I turned to see her and Heather walking over in their fashion show tops and dark jeans.

"Yeah, how do you even know if you're winning?" teased Heather.

I ran toward them and hugged them.

"You guys look great!" I said, squeezing them.

"And you are freakishly strong," grunted Brooke. "Probably why nobody wants to play musical chairs with you."

I let them both go. "Sorry! I'm getting really nervous!"

"It's going to be awesome," Heather assured me. "By the way, Tim's parents really know how to feed a crowd."

She pointed behind us to several buffet tables covered with fruit, cold cuts, crackers, and drinks.

"Oh, you've started referring to yourself as a crowd?" Brooke asked her in an innocent voice. "Sounds about right."

Heather shoved her. "Quiet, or I'm going to eat all those cookies you brought!"

"Which, by the way, are gorgeous!" said Katie, pulling back one of the stage curtains and stepping out. "I want to eat them *and* have them preserved in a museum somewhere." She pointed to me. "Vanny, we need to do a last-minute pep talk with the girls. I hear it's what they always do at Fashion Week."

"Right now?" I asked, looking at the chairs.

"But I'm not done fixing these."

"They're fine, but we can move them around for you," said Brooke.

I rolled my eyes. "No, you can't. You're in the show, remember?" I reached for her and Heather, and the three of us followed Katie backstage.

The rest of the girls in the show were talking and adjusting one another's hair and makeup. When they saw Katie and me, they stopped and stood as still as well-dressed statues.

"Is it time? Is everyone here?" asked Linda in a rushed, excited voice.

"Almost," I said. "First, we just wanted to tell you how grateful we are that you're helping us out. We couldn't have asked for better models."

Katie nodded her agreement. "You're all going to go far. Like to the end of the stage and back."

There was nervous laughter all around.

"The most important thing is to have as much fun wearing these clothes as we did making them." I gestured to Katie, and she smiled.

Brooke cleared her throat and leaned in. "I helped, too."

"Yes!" I put my arms around her and Heather. "All my best friends were there for me, including Tim, who's probably trying to shortchange the audience so he can make more money."

We all laughed again, and it was punctuated by a rhythmic, thumping bass from Berkeley's speakers. I checked my phone. Ten minutes until showtime. And a message from Mom.

Where are you?

I texted her back and flashed my brightest smile at the models. "Good luck out there!"

"Make us proud," added Katie. "Oh! And also start lining up."

While she wrangled the models, I practiced some deep breathing Heather had once taught me.

"Vanessa, honey?" I heard Mom's voice and saw the curtain move in and out.

"Are you really knocking on the curtain before you come in?" I asked with a grin, pulling it back so she could step through.

Mom beamed at me. "My little girl. All grown up and holding a fashion show." She put down the bag she was holding and opened her arms. "The first of many, I might add."

"You got that right," I said, letting her hug me tightly. "Did you bring the stuff I asked for?"

She stepped away from me and picked up the bag. "Bobbi and I had a hard time finding Katie's top, or I would've been here sooner. You want me to stay backstage with you?"

I bit my lip. "I do, but I also want pictures of this whole thing."

Mom chuckled. "Say no more." She kissed my forehead and disappeared through to the other side of the curtain.

Katie came over a moment later. "Aw, I didn't get to say hi to your mom."

"We'll see her after the show. Right now, I want her in the audience taking pictures."

Katie's eyes widened. "Oh, good idea. My mom tends to take pictures of feet and ceilings." She spied the bag I was holding and pulled at one edge. "What's in here?"

I grinned. "Well, remember the other day when you were saying you wished people could see more of our original designs on the runway?" I held open the bag. "I think we can make that happen."

Katie gasped and pulled out a top that I'd seen her make over winter break. "Awesome! Wait. Who's going to wear them? The only people they fit perfectly are us."

I didn't say anything but grinned even wider, and Katie clapped a hand over her mouth and squeaked.

"Unless you don't want to take a turn down the catwalk," I said.

Katie grabbed my shoulders and jumped up and down. "Are you serious? We're going to walk the runway?"

"Only if we can get changed in the next three minutes," I said.

Katie instantly released my shoulders and darted out of sight with her top. I laughed and pulled a shirt I'd made out of the bag, heading for a dressing room. On the way I stopped to peek out from behind the curtain.

The VIP section was entirely full, the first row of girls digging through their swag bags and gushing over the items. Berkeley was off to one side, punching buttons and spinning records while people toward the back filled their plates with *K* and *V* cookies, and fruit. I compared it all to what I'd been planning to do to impress the Lazenby's buyer. Man, it was so much better to be me!

Someone tapped me on the shoulder, and I

turned to see Tim, wearing a headset and carrying a clipboard.

"I'm ready to go whenever you are," he said. On top of his event-planning duties, Tim had also agreed to be the master of ceremonies. He'd definitely earned his money from the VIP sales.

I took a deep breath and clutched my runway top. "It's time. Send out the first girl," I said.

Tim saluted me with his clipboard and spoke into the receiver of his headset as he walked away. The music coming from the speakers shifted tone slightly, but I didn't stick around for Tim's intro. I had a runway to get ready for!

After a tiny incident where I zipped my hair into my top and had to be rescued by a model, I joined Katie behind the curtains. She bounced on the balls of her feet with as much energy as I felt.

"Who's going first? You? Me? Should we go together?" Her hands flew all over the place, like she was feeding a thousand invisible birds.

I grabbed her fingers. "You should go first," I said. "*KV Fashions* starts with a K."

"Good point! Gosh, you are so smart, Vanny. How do I look?" She gave a quick twirl.

"Fabulous. I wouldn't be surprised if someone stole that top the second you changed out of it," I told her with a smile. "But I promise I'd give it back when I was done."

Katie laughed. "Thanks. You don't look too bad yourself!"

"I know," I said, striking a pose.

We both giggled and held nervous, sweaty hands while we waited for the last model to step onto the runway. After a round of applause, Tim's voice boomed out. Even though we'd been expecting it, Katie and I both gave a startled jump and giggled again.

"You've seen the designs," bellowed Tim. "Now see the designers! Introducing either Katie

Kestler or Vanessa Jackson, since I didn't think to ask who was coming out first!"

The audience laughed and clapped. With a final squeeze of my hand, Katie parted the curtain in front of her and stepped out onto the runway. The clapping changed to cheering and whistling, from both sides of the curtain.

Brooke and Heather approached me, having completed their runway walks, both with huge smiles on their faces.

"This is it!" said Brooke. "Time to shine!"

"We're so proud of you!" cheered Heather.

For some reason I felt a little choked up and couldn't trust myself to speak without bawling and ruining my makeup. So I held open my arms, and us Three Musketeers hugged.

"And last but certainly not least," Tim's voice carried over the speakers, "the other half of KV Fashions, Vanessa Jackson!"

Brooke and Heather cheered along with

everyone else, and they held the curtains open for me. Katie was walking in our direction, grinning like mad, and I knew my expression matched hers. We high-fived as she stepped off the stage and I stepped on, and the next thing I knew, all eyes were on me as I strutted down the runway to Tim's description of the design.

Even though I should've been staring straight ahead and doing my best diva pout, I couldn't help sneaking glances at the crowd. They were gazing with admiration at my work, just like I'd always dreamed. Although in my mind I hadn't been the one on the runway.

But just like an iffy acorn-covered top, a dream can always be altered into something better.

Dear A Little Different and other readers,

I was wrong. I know that's not what you want to hear from your advice columnist, but

I wanted to share something I learned from personal experience. Your style is what sets you apart from everyone else. Forget about turning into a new you and wearing more makeup than you're used to. Don't bother with clothes that make you uncomfortable. You don't have to change for anyone. If wearing makeup doesn't feel right, you don't have to wear it. If you're not ready for high fashion yet, no problem! People who like you will like you for who you are. You don't have to do anything but be yourself.

And maybe brush your teeth. You have to have some standards.

Confidentially yours,

Vanessa Jackson

Have you read all the books in the Confidentially Yours series? Turn the page for a sneak peek at the first book!

CHAPTER 1

The Three Musketeers

"Look, I'll show you how to juggle the soccer ball *one* last time," I told Vanessa. "I can't watch you hit yourself in the face again."

"To be fair, I thought we'd be using our hands," she said, rubbing her nose. "And juggling something softer . . . like puppies." A bright pink spot stood out against her skin. If *I'd* been smacked with a soccer ball that many times, my entire face would be as red as my hair.

I tightened my ponytail and took a few steps backward on the school's front lawn. "I'm going to bounce the ball from foot to foot to knee to chest"—I pointed to myself—"and then deflect it to you to hit with your head." I pointed to her. "Got it?"

Vanessa made a face. "Why did I agree to this?" she asked.

"You said you had first-day jitters," I reminded her, balancing the ball on the top of my head. "And the best way to get over them is by distracting your brain. Ready?"

"As I'll ever be," she said, dropping into a squat. Not so graceful for a girl in a wrap skirt, but my fashionista best friend never seemed to care what other people thought. "Come on, Brooke!" she urged me. "School's about to start."

At those words, my arms broke out in goose bumps. Vanessa's jitters had jumped to me . . . but who could blame either of us? This was our first day as middle schoolers!

I shivered with excitement and dropped the ball onto my foot. With the flick of an ankle, it bounced to the other foot, where I popped the ball up waist-high. From there I bounced it on my knee and then leaned back to catch it on my chest. I deflected the ball off me and straight to Vanessa.

Who caught it with her right eye.

"Owww!" She clapped a hand over the side of her face.

"Oh my gosh!" I ran to her. "Are you okay?"

Several kids getting off a bus stopped to stare.

"Theater auditions!" I called to them. "*Ow: The Musical.*"

Vanessa lowered her hand and blinked up at me. "How bad is it?"

"Well . . ." I winced. "Are eye patches in style by any chance?"

She stared at me for a moment and then burst out laughing.

One of the things I love about my best friend? Nothing keeps her down.

"I don't know how you do it, Brooke," she said, rubbing her face. "Soccer's hard . . . especially the ball."

"Awww." I hugged her. "Sorry. I guess I'm just used to it."

"Used to it" was putting it mildly. I've been playing since first grade, and last year I even joined a traveling team, the Berryville Strikers. We came really close to the state championship. This year, that title's ours!

"Maybe you should see the nurse before homeroom," I told Vanessa. "Your face is covered with splotches now."

"Not a problem," she said, reaching into her backpack. She pulled out a slick black case and snapped it open. It was full of eye shadows, blushes, and bronzers.

"I still can't believe your mom agreed to let you wear makeup," I remarked. "You must be the only twelve-year-old in eyeliner."

"I'm pretty sure she got sick of me stealing her stuff," Vanessa said with a grin.

Grabbing a thin makeup brush, she dabbed it in a few colors and swept it across the red spots on her skin. In a matter of seconds, her face was an even mocha tone.

"Amazing."

"I'm still gonna get some ice from the nurse, though," she said, studying her reflection. "I don't want to start middle school as a one-eyed freak."

"At least you'd be on the front page of the *Lincoln Log*," I teased her.

The *Lincoln Log* was our school newspaper . . . one that Vanessa; our other best friend, Heather Schwartz; and I would be working on in our Journalism elective class. We were hoping to get "the Three Musketeers"—our nickname from elementary school—as a byline.

"Don't you dare put me on the front page!"

Vanessa said, narrowing her eyes. She quickly shifted to a smile. "I'd rather be in the style section."

We walked under a giant stone arch with "Abraham Lincoln Middle School" carved into it and stopped just outside the front doors.

"This is it!" said Vanessa with a broad, toothy smile and a nervous bounce. "Sixth grade!"

I nodded and grinned back. "Big things are going to happen for us this year. I can feel it."

"Let the adventure . . . begin!" She pushed on the door.

It didn't budge.

"I think you have to pull," I said.

"Oh." Vanessa yanked on the door handle. "Let the adventure begin!" she repeated.

A rush of unfamiliar sounds, smells, and sights attacked my senses. I tried to find something or someone I recognized while Vanessa hooked her arm through mine.

“Everyone’s so tall,” she whispered, gazing up.

“Maybe we don’t drink enough milk,” I mumbled back. I opened my binder and pulled out a campus map, but Vanessa immediately slapped it out of my hand.

“Don’t let them see that! They’ll think we’re tourists!”

I shot her a confused look. “Huh?”

She shook her head and picked up my map. “Sorry, it’s something my mom says when we’re in Chicago. Defensive reflex.”

I found the nurse’s office on the map, and Vanessa and I braved the crowd in the hallways, stopping just outside the nurse’s door.

“Save me a seat in homeroom!” Vanessa called as I walked away.

“I probably don’t have to!” I shouted back with a grin.

Any time a teacher sat us by last name, it was almost guaranteed that Brooke Jacobs would be sitting behind Vanessa Jackson. The only thing missing?

"Heather!" I called, spotting her outside the music hall. No surprise, considering she's in choir. Vanessa and I are always begging her to sing our favorite songs because her voice is amazing. Like, pop-star-meets-angel amazing.

Heather smiled and waved at me, then went back to her conversation with another dark-haired girl, Gabby Antonides.

I darted through the crowd to join them.

"Hey, guys!"

"Hey!" Heather's voice was soft but excited. "Can you believe we're finally here?"

"No more elementary school. No more pee puddles from the kindergarteners," I said.

Heather giggled. "Or first graders crying when the lights go out."

"Ha! You think it stops there?" asked Gabby. "My brother's still afraid of the dark."

Heather and I laughed.

Gabby's twin brother, Tim, was a giant and a jock. Not exactly the kind of guy you'd expect to need a nightlight.

"So how was your summer?" I asked Gabby.

She rolled her eyes. "Good and bad. I met this cute boy at camp—"

"Good!" I gave a thumbs-up.

"But I kind of lied and said I was the most popular girl in school."

"Bad." I gave a thumbs-down.

"And it turns out he lives in Berryville."

"Worse." I used the thumb to cut off my head.

"Oh, stop," said Heather, bumping me with her hip. "You're scaring Gabby." She took our friend's hands. "You guys don't even go to the same school, so it may never come up. But if it does, tell him the truth and apologize. Say that you were nervous and wanted to impress him."

Gabby's expression grew anxious. "You don't

think he'll hate me?"

"No," Heather said firmly. "There is too much nice about you to hate."

Gabby beamed and hugged her. "I should get going." She waved at us and then ran off.

"I'll never have your knack with people," I told Heather. "But you probably knew that after . . ." I repeated the head-slicing gesture.

She smiled, but held it back just enough to keep her teeth from showing.

Heather is pixie cute but really self-conscious about this teensy-tinesy gap between her front teeth. Vanessa and I have secretly made it our goal to get real smiles out of her all the time.

"First day of school!" I said, trying again.

All Heather did was squeal and grab my hands. "Where's Vanessa?" Heather stood on her tiptoes to peer over the crowd. "She should be with us for this!"

"She went to the nurse's office," I said. "Soccer

ball to the face. Many times."

Heather sighed and shook her head. "That girl needs to design herself a Bubble Wrap wardrobe."

The bell rang, and Heather and I faced each other with wide, excited eyes.

"It's time," I said. "The start of middle school!"

Heather squeezed my hands and squealed again. "Good luck! See you in Journalism!"

"Watch out for hungry eighth graders!" I told her, and darted off to find my homeroom.

Since each grade has its own hallway, it wasn't too hard to find. Plus, our homeroom teacher, Ms. Maxwell, had tacked a huge sign outside her door that said, "Welcome, F through J!"

She was standing in the classroom's entrance with an armful of packets, handing one to each student who entered.

"Good morning!" she said when I stepped closer. "Name?"

"Brooke Jacobs," I said.

"Welcome to Lincoln Middle School, Brooke!" She handed me a packet. "And here is your middle-school survival kit."

"What's inside?" I asked, feeling the weight of it.

"Just some tips about getting the most out of middle school, important dates and room numbers, and information about this year's clubs."

"Clubs? Awesome!" I glanced past her into the classroom. "Um . . . where do I sit?"

Ms. Maxwell held her arms open. "Anywhere you want!"

I staked out two desks in the corner and threw my bag on one of them for Vanessa. After saying a few hellos to the kids I knew, I opened my packet and pulled out the club sheet and a pen, poring over the list.

"Hey! Whatcha doing?" asked Vanessa. She slid into the desk behind me with a wet towel over half her face.

"I'm choosing clubs. What's this about?" I lifted the corner of the towel.

"I'm using a cold compress to reduce swelling," she said. "What clubs are you looking at?"

I handed her the page, and she whistled. "Dang, girl. You circled almost all of these! Art, athletics, band, cooking—"

"I'm hoping they'll let us make pizza."

Pizza is my favorite, pepperoni in particular, and should, in my opinion, be its own food group.

Vanessa kept reading all the way to the end. "Young Sherlocks?"

"I think I'm pretty good at solving mysteries," I said. "Remember that smell in my bedroom? Finally found the source."

She wrinkled her nose. "Well, I, for one, am sticking to whatever will further my fashion career." She frowned. "Which is absolutely nothing on this list."

"What about theater?" I asked. "You could help with costumes and makeup."

Her eyes lit up. "Ooh. Good point!"

I scanned the list. "And Model UN is probably going to want flags or outfits to represent the different countries. Like . . . those overalls and pointy hats for Germany."

"Um . . ." Vanessa wrinkled her forehead. "I'm pretty sure people wear suits for UN meetings."

"Really?" I raised my eyebrows. "I always pictured it like It's a Small World at Disney. How disappointing."

The rest of homeroom and my morning classes (math, PE, and English) went pretty much like elementary school, except with different teachers for each one. And, horror of horrors, homework on the very first day!

At the end of English, every kid in my class scrambled for the cafeteria and our first taste of freedom: lunch. All of sixth grade ate at the same time, while the upper classes ate in later shifts. Probably to spare the sixth graders from ending up in the trash cans.

I found my two best friends, and we claimed a table by the ice-cream cart.

"Middle school is *hard*, you guys," Heather said with a groan. She was in all advanced classes. "In science we're already prepping for our first lab."

"Oooh, what are you doing?" asked Vanessa. "Building a better human?"

Heather smiled at that. "I think we're smashing rocks."

"Too bad," said Vanessa. "Because my classes are seriously lacking in cute guys." She leaned closer. "I think it's so we'll pay more attention."

Heather giggled. "Could be. But I've seen some pretty cute ones in the older grades. Like Stefan Marshall?"

"And Abel Hart," I added. "But we're also

seriously lacking good PE teachers. I need to keep fit for soccer, and an hour of dodgeball isn't exercise!"

"Even though your soccer skills probably make you really good at it," said Heather with a smirk.

"Actually . . . the opposite," I said. "I'm so used to kicking anything that comes at me that I was out in the first two minutes."

Vanessa and Heather looked at each other and then burst out laughing.

"It's not funny!" I said, fighting back a smile.

"So what you really meant," said Vanessa, "was that *watching* an hour of dodgeball isn't exercise."

"Quiet, you!" I threw a grape at her. She deflected it, and it landed in Heather's pudding.

"Hey! I was going to eat that!"

"Like you can't sacrifice one thing on your

tray?" I asked, eyeing Heather's lunch of tuna salad, chips, fruit, pasta, and cake. For a tiny girl, she can seriously chow down. I'm pretty sure she has extra stomachs, like a cow.

We chatted and ate until the bell rang. There was a massive groan from the entire lunchroom, followed by a scraping of chairs on linoleum.

"Journalism time!" I chirped. "*Lincoln Log*, here we come!"

"Save me a seat," said Heather. "I have to get rid of some chocolate pudding that somehow made its way onto my shirt." She narrowed her eyes at Vanessa.

"I'll help," she said with a sheepish grin.

I ventured to class alone, expecting the newsroom to be packed with students, shouting about deadlines and brainstorming ideas. But when I got there, I was only the third person to show.

In the front row a blond girl scribbled like

mad in a notebook. Two rows behind her a guy sat with one long leg resting on top of the desk and the other in the aisle, tapping a beat with his foot.

The girl looked way too frantic to approach, but the guy was doodling a lion, the symbol for Chelsea Football Club, my favorite soccer team. I took it as a sign and sat beside him.

"Chelsea?" I asked.

He blinked at me. "No, I'm Gil."

I laughed. "I meant are you a fan of Chelsea Football Club?" I pointed to his drawing.

"Ohhh!" He laughed too. "No, it's Leo. You know . . . the zodiac sign? I do the horoscopes." Then he returned to his drawing and started bobbing his head to imaginary music.

I settled back in my seat and looked at the white-board while more students strolled in. Different sections and jobs at the paper had been written on the board with names beside them: *editor in chief, features, sports, entertainment, opinion . . .*

I frowned. All the positions were filled. What was left for the Three Musketeers?